Table of Contents

P9-BJY-609

How to Use This Book

This Premium Education Series workbook is designed to suit your teaching needs. Since every child learns at his or her own pace, this workbook can be used individually or as part of small group instruction. The activity pages can be used together with other educational materials and are easily applied to a variety of teaching approaches.

Contents
A detailed table of contents lists all the skills that are covered in the workbook.

Units
The workbook is divided into units of related skills. Numbered tabs allow you to quickly locate each unit. The skills within each unit are designed to be progressively more challenging.

Activity Pages
Each activity page is titled with the skill being practiced or reinforced. The activities and units in this workbook can be used in sequential order, or they can be used to accommodate and supplement any educational curriculum. In addition, the activity pages include simple instructions to encourage independent study, and they are printed in black and white so they can be easily reproduced. Plus, you can record the child's name and the date the activity was completed on each page to keep track of learning progress.

Practice Test
A comprehensive practice test helps prepare the child for standardized testing in a stress-free environment. Presented in the fill-in-the-circle format, this test includes skills covered on standardized tests.

Answer Key
The pages in the back of the workbook provide answers for each activity page as well as the practice test. These answer pages allow you to quickly check the child's work and provide immediate feedback on how he or she is progressing.

Short Vowel Sounds

Name_____ Date_____

a e i o u

Write in the missing vowel to complete each word.

1.  **c__t**	2.  **r__ck**	3.  **m__n**	4.  **d__ck**
5.  **g__m**	6.  **b__t**	7.  **s__ck**	8.  **m__g**
9.  **s__nd**	10.  **p__g**	11.  **h__m**	12. **d__g**
13.  **p__t**	14.  **dr__m**	15.  **p__n**	16.  **p__n**

Name_____ Date_____

Fill in the circle next to the correct word.

1.

○ pin
○ pie

2.
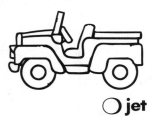
○ jet
○ jeep

3.

○ rack
○ rake

4.

○ male
○ mule

5.

○ leg
○ leaf

6.

○ bike
○ bit

7.

○ globe
○ glue

8.

○ cute
○ cake

9.

○ robe
○ rate

10.

○ tube
○ time

11.

○ bee
○ bell

12.

○ ten
○ team

Long Vowel Sounds (II)

Name_____ Date_____

Write the word that completes each sentence.

dice	goat	juice	mine	paint	peach	toe	tray	try

1. We will help Dad _____ the fence.

2. _____ your best!

3. Roll the _____ to see who goes first.

4. That _____ is ripe and juicy.

5. Put the plate on the _____.

6. Is that cookie _____?

7. The _____ nibbled the grass.

8. Please pour me some orange _____.

9. Ouch! I stubbed my _____ on the rock.

Short and Long Vowel Review

If the word has a short vowel, fill in the circle next to the word **short**.
If the word has a long vowel, fill in the circle next to the word **long**.

1. **bake** ○ a) short ○ b) long	2. **blue** ○ a) short ○ b) long	3. **suit** ○ a) short ○ b) long
4. **jam** ○ a) short ○ b) long	5. **beat** ○ a) short ○ b) long	6. **cub** ○ a) short ○ b) long
7. **chain** ○ a) short ○ b) long	8. **twig** ○ a) short ○ b) long	9. **bump** ○ a) short ○ b) long
10. **snow** ○ a) short ○ b) long	11. **pop** ○ a) short ○ b) long	12. **cheap** ○ a) short ○ b) long
13. **jet** ○ a) short ○ b) long	14. **boat** ○ a) short ○ b) long	15. **crab** ○ a) short ○ b) long
16. **egg** ○ a) short ○ b) long	17. **flute** ○ a) short ○ b) long	18. **crib** ○ a) short ○ b) long
19. **toad** ○ a) short ○ b) long	20. **snack** ○ a) short ○ b) long	21. **lap** ○ a) short ○ b) long
22. **sheep** ○ a) short ○ b) long	23. **hive** ○ a) short ○ b) long	24. **tent** ○ a) short ○ b) long

Vowel Digraphs: oo (I)

Name_____ Date_____

A **vowel digraph** is two vowels put together that stand for one sound. The vowel sound can be short or long.

We t**oo**k a trip to the z**oo**.

Write the word that names each picture.

balloon	boot	broom	goose	igloo	moon
moose	noon	roof	spoon	tools	tooth

1.
_____

2.
_____

3.
_____

4.
_____

5.
_____

6.
_____

7.
_____

8.
_____

9.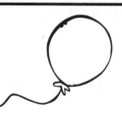
_____

10.
_____

11.
_____

12.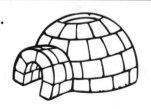
_____

Name_____ Date_____

Write the word that completes each sentence.

| book   cookie   foot   good   hook   look   stood   took   wood |

1. Please hang your jacket on the _____.

2. We _____ in line for a long time.

3. Did you get that _____ from the library?

4. Our family _____ a trip to California.

5. I can hop on one _____.

6. Dad added _____ to the fire.

7. Mmm! That apple pie smells _____!

8. _____ both ways before you cross the street.

9. My dog stole my peanut butter _____!

Vowel Digraphs: ea (1)

Name_____ Date_____

The vowel digraph **ea** can make a short **e** sound.

The cowboy has l**ea**ther boots.

Circle the word that names each picture.

1.	bean	2.	spray	3.	sweater
	breath		spread		sweet
	bread		speed		sweat
4.	streak	5.	head	6.	father
	steak		hard		fatter
	steam		heel		feather

Circle the word that completes each sentence. Write it on the line.

7. Are you _____ to go?   **read**   **ready**

8. My book bag is so _____!   **head**   **heavy**

9. What is the _____ going to be today?   **weather**   **wheat**

10. I like to have eggs for _____.   **bean**   **breakfast**

Name_____ Date_____

Write the word that answers each riddle.

| bread | feathers | healthy | head | heavy |
| leather | meadow | sweater | thread | |

1. You can put me on when it is chilly. _____

2. I am the opposite of light. _____

3. I taste great with peanut butter and jelly. _____

4. I am a kind of material. _____

5. Grandma can sew a patch on with me. _____

6. I am a body part. _____

7. A bird has many of these. _____

8. Eating right, exercise, and rest make you this. _____

9. Animals like to graze in me. _____

Vowel Digraphs: au (I)

Name_____ Date_____

The vowel digraph **au** has a special sound.

Leaves fall in **au**tumn.

Circle the word that has the same vowel sound as the first word.

1.	**auto**	head	cook	date	pause
2.	**sauce**	you	cause	think	sand
3.	**haul**	tail	pool	caught	bead
4.	**aunt**	Paul	night	weight	any
5.	**fault**	good	steak	tulip	because

Write the word that completes each sentence.

6. When will the space shuttle _____?   **launch**   **lunch**

7. Let's _____ this garbage out to the curb.   **heat**   **haul**

8. I _____ my little brother how to play soccer.   **teeth**   **taught**

9. I heard that house is _____.   **haunted**   **hunted**

10. Please put a _____ under the mug.   **saucer**   **settle**

Name_____ Date_____

Write the word that completes each sentence.

August	**autumn**	**caught**	**dinosaur**	**haul**
fault	**launch**	**naughty**	**pause**	

1. The _____ puppy chewed Dad's shoe.

2. _____ is my favorite time of year.

3. When will the rocket _____?

4. It was not my _____ the milk spilled.

5. The scientist will dig for _____ bones.

6. My aunt's birthday is in _____.

7. Grandpa _____ a big fish!

8. Please _____ the movie until everyone is seated.

9. The moving truck will _____ our furniture.

Vowel Digraphs: aw (I)

Name_____ Date_____

The vowel digraph **aw** has a special sound.

The f**aw**n stays near its mother.

Write the word that names each picture.

crawl	draw	hawk	saw	straw	yawn

1.
_____

2.
_____

3.
_____

4.
_____

5.
_____

6.
_____

Write two rhyming words for each word. Use the box if you need help.

7. paw

_____

_____

8. lawn

_____

_____

9. claws

_____

_____

10. yawn

_____

_____

11. saw

_____

_____

12. crawl

_____

_____

bawl	jaws
dawn	laws
draw	pawn
drawn	raw
fawn	shawl
flaw	straw

Vowel Digraphs: aw (II)

Name_____ Date_____

Circle the word that completes each sentence. Write it on the line.

1. The baby _____ was lost in the woods.	**fault** **fawn**
2. We did not cook the meat yet, so it is _____.	**raw** **raised**
3. The bear tore the tent with its sharp _____.	**claws** **cause**
4. Grandma knitted a warm _____.	**shout** **shawl**
5. Paul is _____ a picture of me.	**drawing drinking**
6. The baby is learning to _____.	**clause** **crawl**
7. I _____ you at the movies last night.	**salt** **saw**
8. The kitten has a thorn in its _____.	**paw** **lawn**
9. We stuffed the scarecrow with _____.	**strong** **straw**

Name_____ Date_____

Write the word that completes each sentence.

because	breath	caught	food
jaw saw	scoop	spread	took

1. I _____ a pretty butterfly.

2. Mom will _____ out the blanket.

3. We _____ the solar eclipse yesterday.

4. Jim took a deep _____ before going under water.

5. Give me only one _____ of ice cream.

6. She scraped her _____ when she fell off her bike.

7. The stray cat begged for _____.

8. Our class _____ a field trip to the zoo.

9. Dad took a nap _____ he worked late.

Vowel Digraph Practice (II)

Name_____ Date_____

Fill in the circle next to the word that has the same vowel sound as the first word.

1. **lawn**	○ a) tick	○ b) out	○ c) raw	○ d) tame
2. **mood**	○ a) mud	○ b) roof	○ c) rock	○ d) fork
3. **broom**	○ a) pool	○ b) brook	○ c) caught	○ d) top
4. **thread**	○ a) feet	○ b) bean	○ c) think	○ d) shed
5. **shook**	○ a) took	○ b) spool	○ c) your	○ d) fault
6. **bawl**	○ a) ten	○ b) awesome	○ c) cake	○ d) catch
7. **vault**	○ a) taunt	○ b) calf	○ c) vanish	○ d) village
8. **flaw**	○ a) flee	○ b) paw	○ c) rich	○ d) cabin
9. **head**	○ a) leaf	○ b) heat	○ c) shake	○ d) wealth
10. **look**	○ a) boot	○ b) you	○ c) stood	○ d) cute
11. **taught**	○ a) rate	○ b) launch	○ c) tune	○ d) table
12. **school**	○ a) chalk	○ b) tub	○ c) snooze	○ d) job

Name_____ Date_____

A **diphthong** is two letters blended together to make one special vowel sound.

The kangaroo likes to b<u>ou</u>nce.

Write the word that names each picture.

blouse	cloud	couch	count	hound
house	mouse	mouth	south	

1. _____

2. _____

3. _____

4. _____

5. _____

6. _____

7. _____

8. _____

9. _____

Write a word from the word box that is the opposite.

found	grouchy	out	pout	shout	sour

10. whisper _____

11. sweet _____

12. happy _____

13. lost _____

14. in _____

15. smile _____

Name_____ Date_____

Write the word that completes each sentence.

bounce	found	ground	loud	mouse
our	pouch	sound	loud	sprout

1. That music is too _____!

2. _____ class studied the Rain Forest.

3. The little gray _____ ate the cheese.

4. John can _____ the ball high.

5. A baby kangaroo stays in its mother's _____.

6. The airplane landed safely on the _____.

7. A tiny plant is beginning to _____.

8. What made that funny _____?

9. Tara _____ a quarter at the park.

Diphthongs: ow (I)

Name_____ Date_____

The letters **ow** can stand for the vowel sound in cl<u>ow</u>n or the long o sound in b<u>ow</u>.

Color the picture if the word has the vowel sound in **clown**.
Circle **long o** if it has the sound in **bow**.

1. long o **row**	2. long o **gown**	3. long o **town**
4. long o **snow**	5. long o **crown**	6. long o **throw**
7. long o **cow**	8. long o **mow**	9. long o **frown**
10. long o **flower**	11. long o **crow**	12. long o **towel**

Diphthongs: ow (II)

Name_____ Date_____

Write the word that completes each sentence.

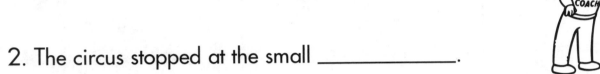

blow	down	growl	how	know	plow	show	tow	town

1. Did you hear the coach _____ the whistle?

2. The circus stopped at the small _____.

3. A _____ truck pulled our car to the station.

4. _____ do you get to your house?

5. The boy could not climb _____ from the tree.

6. Does she _____ how to swim?

7. The dancers put on a great _____!

8. Did that big dog _____ at you?

9. The farmer must _____ his wheat field.

Diphthongs: oi and oy (1)

Name_____ Date_____

The **oi** in c**oi**ns and the **oy** in b**oy** have the same sound.

Unscramble the letters. Write the **oi** or **oy** word from the box that names each picture.

boy foil toy point coins Roy

1. **l i f o**

_____

2. **o y t**

_____

3. **n o i c s**

_____

4. **o R y**

_____

5. **t n o p i**

_____

6. **y o b**

_____

Write the word that completes each sentence.

7. Please _____ us in singing a song.

8. Did you _____ the show?

9. Mom will _____ the water for the noodles.

10. Stop making all that _____!

boil
enjoy
join
noise

Diphthongs: oi and oy (II)

Name_____ Date_____

Write **oi** or **oy** to complete each word in the sentence.

1. The b_____ p_____nts to the funny clown.

2. R_____ will j_____n the basketball team.

3. The baby enj_____s her new t_____.

4. I saved ten dollars and a few c_____ns.

5. We planted the tree in the m_____st s_____l.

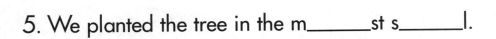

6. Did you make a good ch_____ce?

7. The r_____al king ate a br_____led steak.

8. The loud n_____se is really ann_____ing!

9. My friend J_____ has a nice singing v_____ce.

Diphthongs: ew (1)

Name_____ Date_____

The **ew** in scr**ew**  has the long **u** sound.

Write the word that completes each sentence.

| blew | brew | chew | drew | few | flew | grew | knew | threw |

1. Eric _____ a big bubble.

2. In the winter, the birds _____ south.

3. The smell from the witch's _____ filled the air.

4. She already _____ how to solve the math problems.

5. The big dog likes to _____ on rawhide bones.

6. I only have a _____ pieces of candy left.

7. Jack's beanstalk _____ up to the sky.

8. The pitcher _____ three strikes to the batter.

9. The teacher _____ a square on the chalkboard.

Diphthongs: ew (II)

Name_____ Date_____

Fill in the circle next to the word that completes each sentence.

1. Drew wanted a ____ pet.　　　　　　　　　　　○ a) blew　　○ b) new

2. He looked at a ____ different animals.　　　　○ a) few　　　○ b) pew

3. Finally, he found a kitten and named her ____.　○ a) Mew　　○ b) flew

4. Drew couldn't wait to tell his Dad the ____.　　○ a) hew　　○ b) news

5. He ____ she would love her new home.　　　　○ a) stew　　○ b) knew

6. In a ____ days Mew knew her way around.　　　○ a) few　　　○ b) new

7. She liked to ____ on Mom's yarn.　　　　　　○ a) chew　　○ b) grew

8. Drew fed her some yummy ____.　　　　　　○ a) dew　　　○ b) stew

9. She liked to hide under the ____.　　　　　　○ a) slew　　○ b) newspaper

10. Mew chased leaves when the wind ____.　　　○ a) blew　　○ b) chew

11. She would jump to catch a toy when Drew ____ it.　○ a) brew　　○ b) threw

12. One day she stepped on a sharp ____.　　　　○ a) dew　　　○ b) screw

13. A whole ____ of veterarians wrapped her paw.　○ a) crew　　○ b) drew

14. Mew ____ bigger and bigger every day.　　　　○ a) grew　　○ b) flew

15. Drew loved his ____ pet!　　　　　　　　　○ a) knew　　○ b) new

Diphthong Practice (1)

Name_____ Date_____

Write the word that completes each sentence.

blew	bow	coin	crown	knew	loud	noise	our	owl

1. The crowd gave a _____ cheer.

2. Troy dropped a _____ in the gumball machine.

3. The wind _____ the leaves all over the yard.

4. _____ town is having a homecoming parade.

5. Mom tied a _____ in her hair.

6. That loud _____ scared the baby.

7. A wise _____ watched from the top of the tree.

8. Grandpa _____ how to fix the broken door.

9. The queen wore her royal _____ proudly.

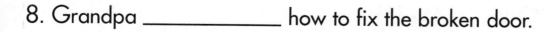

Diphthong Practice (II)

Name_____ Date_____

Fill in the circle next to the word that has the same vowel sound as the first word.

1. **toy**	○ a) knew	○ b) awful	○ c) joy	○ d) glow
2. **bound**	○ a) shout	○ b) noise	○ c) boy	○ d) snow
3. **low**	○ a) power	○ b) blew	○ c) grow	○ d) voice
4. **few**	○ a) our	○ b) threw	○ c) now	○ d) enjoy
5. **trout**	○ a) foil	○ b) row	○ c) dew	○ d) south
6. **cloud**	○ a) frown	○ b) boil	○ c) tow	○ d) would
7. **coil**	○ a) how	○ b) soy	○ c) found	○ d) glow
8. **chew**	○ a) spoil	○ b) town	○ c) new	○ d) row
9. **ounce**	○ a) coy	○ b) stew	○ c) our	○ d) moist
10. **crew**	○ a) ground	○ b) plow	○ c) soil	○ d) shoe
11. **broil**	○ a) toy	○ b) slow	○ c) couch	○ d) shrewd
12. **blew**	○ a) voice	○ b) mow	○ c) grew	○ d) sound

R-controlled Vowels: ar (1)

Name_____ Date_____

The words m**ar**ch and st**ar**t have the same vowel sound.

Circle the word that names each picture.

1.  aim **arm**	2.  pack **park**	3.  **star** stay
4.  make **mark**	5.  **harp** hand	6.  **party** pantry
7.  come **card**	8.  yawn **yard**	9.  **yarn** yak
10.  **farm** from	11.  corn **car**	12.  **jar** jacks

Name_____ Date_____

Write the word that completes each sentence.

cart	charm	chart	dark	far	harm	shark	sharp	smart

1. I lost Grandma's _____ bracelet.

2. Be careful, that knife is _____.

3. The _____ swam through the ocean waters.

4. Eating too much candy may _____ your teeth.

5. We put our groceries into the _____.

6. In the _____ forest, the animals slept peacefully.

7. The doctor asked me to read an eye _____.

8. How _____ is it to California?

9. You are so _____!

Name_____ Date_____

The words g**er**m, f**ir**st, and b**ur**n all have the same vowel sound.

Circle the word that names each picture.

1.  **barn bird**	2.  **worm warm**	3.  **trip turn**
4.  **fern farm**	5.  **earth eat**	6.  **drip dirt**
7.  **shup shirt**	8.  **clack clerk**	9. **squirm squirrel**
10.  **star stir**	11.  **girl glad**	12.  **nurse nerve**

Circle the words that have the same vowel sound as in **lear**n.

14.   germ   circus   arm   hear   firm   birthday   tear

15.   four   fur   turtle   fear   hurt   skirt   cherry

Name_____ Date_____

Write the word that completes each sentence.

| batter | curl | dirt | hurt | letter | skirt | squirts | thirty | twirl |

1. I wrote a _____ to my friend.

2. That building is _____ years old.

3. The _____ hit a homerun.

4. My sister likes to _____ my hair.

5. She spilled juice on her new _____.

6. The dancers _____ around and around.

7. The fireman _____ water on the burning house.

8. Joey _____ his knee while riding his skateboard.

9. The boy dug a hole in the _____.

Name_____ Date_____

Unit 1

The words sh**or**t and sp**or**ts have the same vowel sound.

Circle the word that names each picture.

1.

cook   cork

2.

orange   otter

3.

stork   stock

4.

hose   horse

5.

stare   store

6.

corn   cone

7.

foot   fork

8.

snore   story

9.

hungry   horn

10.

star   storm

11.

forest   fort

12.

thirst   thorn

R-controlled Vowels: or (II)

Name_____ Date_____

Write the word that completes each sentence.

chores fort more porch pork scored short sword wore

1. We made a _____ in our tree.

2. She _____ her best dress to the show.

3. The old man rested on the _____.

4. That restaurant has the best _____ chops!

5. The pirate used his _____ to fight off the shark.

6. May I have some _____ juice please?

7. Jim _____ the winning goal in the soccer game.

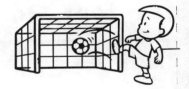

8. After I do my _____, I can play outside.

9. The kite string is too _____.

Premium Education Language Arts: Grade 2   **32**   © Learning Horizons

Name_____ Date_____

Write the word that answers each riddle.

| chirp | farm | first | fork | hard | nurse | river | shark | turtle |

1. I am the same as a stream. _____

2. I am the opposite of last. _____

3. You can eat with me. _____

4. I carry my house on my back. _____

5. This is the sound a bird makes. _____

6. I live in the ocean and have sharp teeth. _____

7. This is a place where crops are grown. _____

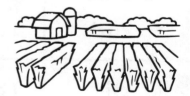

8. The opposite of soft. _____

9. I can help you when you are sick. _____

R-controlled Vowel Practice (II)

Name_____ Date_____

Fill in the circle next to the word that has the same vowel sound as the first word.

1. **park**	○ a) form	○ b) cart	○ c) thirty	○ d) plate
2. **fur**	○ a) fruit	○ b) your	○ c) fork	○ d) during
3. **fern**	○ a) learn	○ b) lean	○ c) listen	○ d) land
4. **third**	○ a) turn	○ b) tip	○ c) rust	○ d) pork
5. **torn**	○ a) moth	○ b) toe	○ c) storm	○ d) thought
6. **cord**	○ a) frost	○ b) chirp	○ c) candy	○ d) port
7. **march**	○ a) hard	○ b) moist	○ c) middle	○ d) cloth
8. **spurt**	○ a) nuts	○ b) burn	○ c) moss	○ d) snore
9. **curb**	○ a) shirt	○ b) cute	○ c) barge	○ d) tune
10. **stir**	○ a) brush	○ b) stiff	○ c) thick	○ d) clerk
11. **harp**	○ a) handy	○ b) scarf	○ c) shake	○ d) huge
12. **horn**	○ a) roof	○ b) burn	○ c) sport	○ d) home

Two-Letter Blends

Name_____ Date_____

A **consonant blend** is two or more consonants put together.
The sounds are blended together and each sound is heard.

A **sm**all squirrel **sc**attered nuts on the **gr**ound.

Circle the word that names each picture.

1.  plant prince	2.  grip glove	3.  bride block	4.  blimp brush	5. crab clam
6.  clip crown	7.  swim sling	8. step spoon	9. smile snail	10.  scale skate
11. frog flip	12.  door drip	13.  cricket clock	14.  sting sled	15. crib clown
16.  blink broom	17. spark star	18.  tree tar	19. grape glue	20. flag frown

Three-Letter Blends

Name_____ Date_____

Write the word that names each picture.

| screw | scrub | spray | spring | squirrel | straw | string | strong |

1.  _____	2.  _____	3.  _____	4. _____
5.  _____	6.  _____	7.  _____	8.  _____

Complete each sentence using one of the words from above.

9. My muscles are big and _____.

10. We need a _____ to hang the picture.

11. Flowers begin to bloom in the _____.

12. The furry _____ gathered nuts.

Ending Blends

Name_____ Date_____

Write the word that names each picture.

band	chick	desk	fist	hand	king	plant	ring
sand	sing	skunk	swing	tent	truck	wand	wing

1.
_____

2.
_____

3.
_____

4.
_____

5.
_____

6.
_____

7.
_____

8.
_____

9.
_____

10.
_____

11.
_____

12.
_____

13.
_____

14.
_____

15.
_____

16.
_____

Name_____ Date_____

Circle the word that completes each sentence. Write it on the line.

1. Patty plays the _____ in the band.	**tray**	**flute**
_____		
2. The scouts folded the _____ proudly.	**flag**	**glue**
_____		
3. The three billy goats crossed the _____.	**bridge**	**clam**
_____		
4. Tom Sawyer built a _____ from logs.	**raft**	**toast**
_____		
5. A smelly _____ snuck into our tent.	**scale**	**skunk**
_____		
6. Brad put fifty cents in his _____.	**bank**	**tree**
_____		
7. The _____ rode on a gray horse.	**prince**	**grape**
_____		
8. Mom will _____ the fresh oranges.	**stripe**	**squeeze**
_____		
9. The fire caused a lot of _____.	**snail**	**smoke**

Blend Practice

Name_____ Date_____

Circle the blend in each word and write it on the line.

1. prize _____

2. glass _____

3. fruit _____

4. cloud _____

5. drum _____

6. dress _____

7. wink _____

8. lamp _____

9. smile _____

10. bring _____

11. glad _____

12. train _____

13. mask _____

14. stir _____

15. strawberry _____

16. slide _____

17. sled _____

18. milk _____

19. screw _____

20. snap _____

21. west _____

Write the word that answers each riddle.

22. You can turn me on for light. _____

23. You can sleep in me. _____

24. I make people laugh. _____

25. I am the opposite of go. _____

| clown |
| lamp |
| stop |
| tent |

Digraphs: ch and sh

Name_____ Date_____

A **consonant digraph** is two consonants put together that make one sound. They can be found at the beginning or at the end of a word.

She made a wi**sh** for a bun**ch** of **ch**eese!

Write **ch** or **sh** to complete each word.

1. ____**air**	2. **fi**____	3. ____**eck**	4. ____**ief**
5.  **bran**____	6.  ____**est**	7. ____**oe**	8.  **bu**____
9. **tea**____**er**	10. ____**ark**	11. ____**irt**	12.  **in**____
13. **di**____	14. **fla**____	15.  ____**ur**____	16. ____**apes**
17. ____**ain**	18.  **tra**____	19.  **ben**____	20. ____**op**

Digraphs: th and wh

Name_____ Date_____

The **wh**ite **wh**ale lost a too**th**.

Write **th** or **wh** to complete each word.

1. ____ imble	2. ____ eel	3.  too____	4.  ____ ale
5.  mo ____ er	6. ____ ree	7.  ____ umb	8.  ____ eat

Circle the word that completes each sentence. Write it on the line.

9. The old TV show is in black and _____.	**where** **white**
10. I _____ I can do these problems.	**then** **think**
11. Can you tell _____ answer is right?	**which** **wheat**
12. I pricked my thumb on the _____ bush.	**that** **thorn**

Name_____ Date_____

Ph has the same sound as **f**.

p̲hone

Circle the word that names the picture.

1. **author** **A, B, C...** **alphabet**	2. **shovel** **elephant**
3. **pheasant** **fiddle**	4. **graph** **photo**
5. **trophy** **tooth**	6. **gopher** **first**

Write the word that completes each sentence.

7. Our teacher gave a _____ lesson.

8. The _____ haunted the old house.

9. That diamond is a _____.

10. _____ is a city in Pennsylvania.

11. Mom works at the _____.

12. The _____ took our picture.

phantom
pharmacy
Philadelphia
phonics
photographer
phony

Name_____ Date_____

In some words, **gh** has the sound of **f**.
In other words, **gh** is silent—it makes no sound. **laugh**

light

Write the word that completes each sentence.

cough	fight	high	laugh	light
right	rough	thought	through	

1. She has a cold with a _____.

2. Please turn off the _____ when you're done.

3. I _____ it was the best book I ever read!

4. The plane flew up _____.

5. Turn the car to the _____.

6. "Do not _____ with your brothers!" yelled Mom.

7. The silly clown made us _____.

8. Tree bark feels _____, not smooth.

9. The boy will go all the way _____ the tunnel.

Name_____ Date_____

Read the story. Fill in the missing letters.

| ch | sh | th | wh | gh | ph | ng |

Bear sat in a ____air. The tele____one began to
     1.   2.

ri____. It was Bear's friend, ____imp. "A ____eel fell off my
 3.   4.   5.

bike!" said ____imp. "I ____ink I can fix it," said Bear.
         6.   7.

"I will come over to your house." "____en?" asked ____imp.
                                  8.   9.

"Ri____t now!" said Bear. "I will bri____ my tools." It took Bear
   10.   11.

only a ____ort time to fix the ____eel. "____is ____eel is on
     12.   13.   14.   15.

nice and ti____t now," said Bear.
        16.

"____ank you!" said ____imp
 17.   18.

and he ____ook Bear's hand.
    19.

Silent Letters (1)

Name_____ Date_____

In words beginning with **gn** or **kn**,
the **k** or **g** is silent and only the **n** is heard.

knee

In words beginning with **wr**,
the **w** is silent and only the **r** is heard.

wrist

In words ending with **mb**,
the **b** is usually silent and only the **m** is heard.

co**mb**

Write the word that names each picture.

comb	gnaw	knee	knock	knot	lamb
thumb	wrap	wren	wring	wrist	write

1.

_____

2.

_____

3.

_____

4.

_____

5.

_____

6.

_____

7.

_____

8.

_____

9.

_____

10.

_____

11.

_____

12.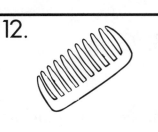

_____

Name_____ Date_____

Write the word that completes each sentence.

| climb | crumb | gnome | knew | knot |
| knight | wrench | write | wrong | |

1. Mom has a statue of a _____ in her garden.

2. The bus driver stopped at the _____ corner.

3. The brave _____ fought the enemy.

4. Did you ever _____ to the top of a mountain?

5. Dad used the _____ to fix the leaky pipe.

6. The little mouse ate the cracker _____.

7. Please _____ your name at the top of the paper.

8. Greg _____ all the answers!

9. My shoe string has a _____.

Name_____ Date_____

Unit 2

Fill in the circle next to the word that has the same beginning sound as the first word.

1. **wheel**	○ a) thistle	○ b) cheap	○ c) white	○ d) shop
2. **three**	○ a) sheep	○ b) think	○ c) where	○ d) time
3. **photo**	○ a) shark	○ b) father	○ c) thin	○ d) chop
4. **knock**	○ a) nickel	○ b) shine	○ c) wheat	○ d) kettle
5. **cherry**	○ a) tooth	○ b) clam	○ c) chin	○ d) ship
6. **shy**	○ a) shell	○ b) sky	○ c) chute	○ d) that
7. **wrap**	○ a) wand	○ b) whistle	○ c) thick	○ d) ring
8. **which**	○ a) wren	○ b) water	○ c) whip	○ d) chip

Cross out the letter or letters in each word that are silent.

9. might   10. wrong   11. high   12. through   13. lamb

14. gnaw   15. knob   16. light   17. gnat   18. tight

19. wrist   20. crumb   21. sight   22. knife   23. write

Name_____ Date_____

The first word in a sentence is always capitalized.

<u>T</u>he cow grazed in the meadow.

Circle each word that should begin with a capital letter.

one sunny morning, Jimmy woke up to the sound of roosters

crowing. he jumped out of bed and ran downstairs. his mother fixed

him a bowl of cereal for breakfast. after breakfast, Jimmy had to do

his chores on the farm. first he milked the cows. then he fed the pigs

and gave them fresh water. next he gathered eggs from the chickens.

finally, his work was done.

Write two sentences about the picture. Don't forget the capitals!

1. _____

_____

2. _____

_____

Name_____ Date_____

The word **I** and names of people and pets are always capitalized.

I have a pet skunk. His name is **S**tinky.

Circle each word that should begin with a capital letter.

kate wanted a pet. She looked at every pet store and finally decided on a skunk. "i will name him stinky," she said. stinky was a very friendly skunk. He liked to hop around the yard and chew on the flowers. One day stinky met a strange dog. It was sniffer, the neighbor's dog. kate said, "i hope the two of you can be friends." Then the two animals ran off to play together.

Write two sentences about your favorite pet or animal.
Be sure to give it a name.

1. _____

_____

2. _____

_____

Name_____ Date_____

A sentence that tells something is a **statement**.
A **period** is used at the end of a statement.

We saw a dinosaur at the museum.

Read the story. Add a period at the end of each statement.
There are seven periods missing.

Our class took a trip to the museum We saw all kinds of dinosaurs I felt like a mouse standing next to those huge models My favorite was the brontosaurus I wished I could've rode on its tail The teacher took our picture with a life-size raptor It was fun learning about the dinosaurs

Write two statements about a trip you have taken.

1. _____

_____

2. _____

_____

Statements (II)

Name_____ Date_____

Fill in the circle next to each statement that is written correctly.

○ 1. Last summer, we took a trip to the beach.

○ 2. We stayed in a hotel with a great view of the ocean

○ 3. there was so much to do.

○ 4. I love the how the warm sand feels under my toes

○ 5. We buried Dad in sand up to his neck.

○ 6. my little sister searched for seashells

○ 7. We found some clams that were washed up on shore.

○ 8. The ocean water was cool and salty.

○ 9. The big waves were fun to jump in

○ 10. my brother even learned how to surf.

○ 11. Mom enjoyed relaxing in the sun and reading her favorite book.

○ 12. I can't wait to go back to the beach again someday

Commands

Name_____ Date_____

A **command** is a sentence that gives directions or orders. Every command ends with a **period**.

Clean your room**.**

Fill in the circle next to each sentence that is a command.

○ 1. The ballerina danced gracefully.

○ 2. Don't touch the hot stove.

○ 3. Wear your helmet.

○ 4. Add two cups of sugar.

○ 5. He kicked the soccer ball.

○ 6. Close the door.

○ 7. She doesn't like to eat peas.

○ 8. The clouds are gray.

○ 9. Put your name on your paper.

○ 10. I like to walk in the park.

Name_____ Date_____

Sentences that ask something are called **questions**.
Every question sentence ends with a **question mark**.

Did you see that shooting star**?**

Read the story. Add a question mark at the end of each question.
There are six question marks missing.

Unit 3

Josh and his best friend Tommy were camping out in the backyard. As they were starring into the star filled sky they noticed a shooting star. "What do you think that was " asked Josh. "I think it was a spaceship," said Tommy. "Do you think we should check it out " Josh asked. Tommy replied, "Yes, maybe there are aliens." So the two boys searched for the fallen object. "What if there <u>are</u> aliens " Tommy wondered. "What would they look like How would they speak What if they took us into their spaceship " Then all of a sudden, the boys fell asleep.

Write two questions about the picture.

1. _____

_____

2. _____

_____

Name_____ Date_____

Fill in the circle next to each question that is written correctly.

○ 1. What is your phone number?

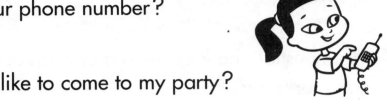

○ 2. Would you like to come to my party?

○ 3. what is your favorite ice cream?

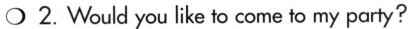

○ 4. How old are you.

○ 5. Is that your puppy?

○ 6. Do you like to jump rope.

○ 7. Who is that knocking on the door?

○ 8. can I go to the park?

○ 9. did you see that new video game?

○ 10. May I have some popcorn?

Exclamations

Name_____ Date_____

Sentences that show excitement or strong feelings are called **exclamations**, or exclamatory sentences. Exclamations end with an **exclamation point**.

What a great ride**!**

Read the story. Add exclamation points at the end of each exclamation. There are six exclamation points missing.

I love going to amusement parks My favorite ride is the roller coaster. Every time the train gets to the top of the hill, my heart begins to pound. Woosh The track clatters and wind flies through my hair. Look out I feel like I'm going to fly out of my seat Soon we're back at the station. Wow What a thrill It was so much fun.

_____

Write two exclamations about the picture.

1. _____

_____

2. _____

_____

Proofreading for Punctuation

Name_____ Date_____

Read the story. Add the missing ending punctuation marks. There are eleven missing periods, three missing question marks, and six missing exclamation points.

Zachary and his Grandpa went fishing__ "Is this a good spot Grandpa__" asked Zachary.

"Perfect__" Grandpa said.

They began to cast their reels__ Then Zachary noticed a sign. It read: No Fishing__ Keep Out__

"Rats__" cried Grandpa. "We'll have to go down the river a little farther," he said. Suddenly they came to the perfect spot__ "Ahhh__" This is great__" cried Grandpa__ "Do you need help baiting your hook__" he asked.

"No, I can do it," Zachary answered__

They cast their fishing lines into the water and waited. Grandpa told some stories while they ate a picnic lunch. Then Zachary felt something pulling on his line__ "Oh, I think I got one__" he yelled. As he reeled in his line, the big fish tugged and tugged. "Help, Grandpa__" he screamed. Together they reeled in the big fish. But when Zachary looked, there was nothing on the end of the hook__ "What happened__" he asked.

Grandpa replied, "That's the big one that got away__"

Name_____ Date_____

Unit 3

Fill in the circle next to each sentence that is written correctly.

○ 1. mom planted a vegetable garden.

○ 2. Karen plays the flute in the school band.

○ 3. Ouch! I got stung by a big bee!

○ 4. Do the dishes.

○ 5. Harry is my pet spider.

○ 6. the little baby cried loudly.

○ 7. The teacher hung my picture on the board?

○ 8. When will your Dad be home?

○ 9. My sister likes to shop for shoes.

○ 10. The dragon breathed fire at the princess?

Common Nouns

Common nouns name any person, place, thing, or idea.

The **dog** chewed on a **bone**.

Circle all the common nouns in each sentence.

1. A frog caught a fly on its tongue.

2. Grandma sent a basket of cookies.

3. David played a game on the computer.

4. The girl rode her bike to the store.

5. Mom cooked chicken and rice.

6. My kitten likes to play with the yarn.

7. The truck raced down the street.

8. A man built the deck in four days.

9. Caterpillars turn into butterflies.

10. The doctor gave the lady some medicine.

Proper Nouns

Proper nouns name a special person, place, thing, or idea. Proper nouns always begin with a capital letter.

Mrs. Thomas went to **Kansas City**.

Circle the proper noun in each sentence. Rewrite it correctly.

1. The house on cherry street is for sale. _____

2. chicago is a great place to visit. _____

3. jeremy likes to play golf. _____

4. The game was played at central school. _____

5. mr. turner has a new car. _____

6. We will visit her grandma on friday. _____

7. The pacific ocean is the largest ocean. _____

8. The memorial day parade starts at 9:00. _____

9. My dad likes to ski in the month of december. _____

Unit 3

Nouns in Context

Name_____ Date_____

Write the best noun to complete each sentence.

bananas	fish	giraffes	hay	kangaroos	Mrs. Smith	April
picnic	pictures	plants	pool	Rain Forest	rocks	rope	School

Last _____ our class took a trip to the zoo. We saw
1.

many different animals. The elephants nibbled on _____. The
2.

_____ stretched their long necks. Lazy lions slept on
3.

_____. The polar bears swam in their _____.
4.   5.

_____, our teacher fed the sea lions some smelly
6.

_____. We watched the silly monkeys swing from the
7.

_____ and eat _____. Our class saw
8.   9.

Australian _____ that bounced all over. The
10.

_____ was a special exhibit. The _____
11.   12.

and birds were all so beautiful! Later we had a _____
13.

lunch. When we got back to Washington _____, we drew
14.

_____ of our favorite animal.
15.

Plural Nouns (I)

Name_____ Date_____

Nouns that show more than one are called **plural nouns**. Add **s** to most nouns to show more than one. For nouns ending in **sh**, **ch**, **x**, **s**, **ss**, and **z**, add **es** to show more than one.

Look at the two dog**s**.

Look at the two fox**es**.

Add **s** or **es** to make each noun plural. Write the plural word on the line.

Unit 3

1. bell _____

2. bus _____

3. truck _____

4. kitten _____

5. box _____

6. peach _____

7. egg _____

8. lunch _____

9. boot _____

10. cup _____

11. dress _____

12. dish _____

13. pencil _____

14. girl _____

15. hat _____

16. wish _____

17. mix _____

18. tree _____

Plural Nouns (II)

Name_____ Date_____

Some nouns end in **y** after a consonant. To make these nouns plural, change the **y** to **i** and add **es**.

one bunny   bunn**y** + es = bunnies   two bunnies

Rewrite each noun to make it plural.

1. candy _____

2. baby _____

3. lady _____

4. cherry _____

5. puppy _____

6. fly _____

7. berry _____

8. daisy _____

9. city _____

10. bunny _____

Circle the correct word to complete each sentence.

11. Mom bought two quarts of (**berry**, **berries**).

12. We drove into the (**city**, **cities**).

13. The (**fly**, **flies**) keeps buzzing in my ear.

14. The (**lady**, **ladies**) talked about the book.

15. I picked a bunch of (**daisy**, **daisies**) for my teacher.

Possessive Nouns

Name_____ Date_____

To show a person or thing owns something is called showing **possession**. If the noun names just one, add an **apostrophe** and an **s**. If the noun names more than one, just add an **apostrophe**.

<u>One</u>
one dog's tail

<u>More Than One</u>
two dogs' tails

Circle the noun that shows possession correctly. Write it on the line.

1. Did I hear one _____ whistle?

coach's   coaches'

2. Two _____ outfits are pink.

dancer's   dancers'

3. Look at that _____ costume.

boy's   boys'

4. Both _____ caps blew away.

player's   players'

5. That one is my _____ desk.

teacher's teachers'

6. The _____ bike has two wheels.

girl's   girls'

7. Many _____ homes were destroyed in the fire.

animal's   animals'

8. _____ car needs to be washed.

Dad's   Dads'

Pronouns (I)

Name_____ Date_____

Pronouns are words that take the place of other nouns.

Pronouns in the Subject	Pronouns in the Predicate
I	me
we	us
he, she, they	him, her, them

Circle the correct pronoun that could take the place of the underlined word or words.

1. <u>Tony</u> named the pet hamster Porky.	**I** **Me**
2. <u>Our family</u> had a picnic in the park.	**We** **Us**
3. Sara showed <u>Rachel</u> how to play the game.	**she** **her**
4. Mom drove <u>Jim and Larry</u> home.	**we** **us**
5. <u>Ian</u> is in second grade.	**He** **Him**
6. We saw <u>our friends</u> at the carnival.	**they** **them**
7. Mr. Jones gave <u>Beth</u> a dollar.	**she** **her**

Pronouns (II)

Name_____ Date_____

Circle the correct pronoun to complete each sentence.

1. (**I, Me**) am the winner of the writing contest!

2. The fairy gave (**he, him**) three wishes.

3. (**They, Them**) came to the birthday party.

4. (**She, Her**) skates fast.

5. Mom read a story to (**I, me**).

6. The clown did a trick for (**we, us**).

7. The coach gave (**them, they**) a smile.

8. (**We, Us**) played a game of tennis.

9. The teacher gave (**them, they**) a treat.

10. My pet came with (**I, me**) to the park.

11. The store owner gave (**we, us**) a piece of candy.

12. (**Her, She**) is my sister's friend.

Unit 3

Plural Noun Practice

Name_____ Date_____

Fill in the circle next to the word that shows the correct plural of the noun.

1. **daisy**	2. **book**	3. **girl**	4. **paper**	5. **snake**
○ a) daisys	○ a) books	○ a) girls	○ a) paperes	○ a) snakes
○ b) daisies	○ b) bookes	○ b) girles	○ b) papers	○ b) snaks
6. **puppy**	7. **fox**	8. **bike**	9. **chair**	10. **brush**
○ a) puppys	○ a) foxes	○ a) biks	○ a) chaires	○ a) brushes
○ b) puppies	○ b) foxs	○ b) bikes	○ b) chairs	○ b) brushs
11. **towel**	12. **city**	13. **class**	14. **pickle**	15. **chick**
○ a) towels	○ a) citys	○ a) class's	○ a) pickles	○ a) chicks
○ b) toweles	○ b) cities	○ b) classes	○ b) picklees	○ b) chickes
16. **bean**	17. **lunch**	18. **boat**	19. **teacher**	20. **flash**
○ a) beanes	○ a) lunches	○ a) boates	○ a) teachers'	○ a) flashes
○ b) beans	○ b) lunchs	○ b) boats	○ b) teachers	○ b) flashs

Adjectives

Adjectives tell more about nouns.
Some **adjectives** answer these questions:

What kind?

How many?

What color?

Circle two adjectives in each sentence.

1. Red fish swim beside green seaweed.

2. One clam sits on the tan sand.

3. Nosy eels look into the old ship.

4. Can you see the gold coins in the open chest?

5. Three happy seahorses play by the ship.

6. Surprises wait under the cool, blue sea.

7. Shiny, green seaweed grows at the bottom.

8. Many fish blow big bubbles.

Adjectives that Compare

Name_____ Date_____

Adjectives can be used to compare things. Add **er** to an adjective when you compare two things. Add **est** to an adjective when you compare three or more things.

tall   **taller**   **tallest**

Write the correct adjective to complete each sentence.

1. A race car is _____, but an airplane is _____.	**fast** **faster**
2. We saw a _____ mouse than before, but this one is the _____.	**smallest** **smaller**
3. My hair is _____, but Julie's is the _____.	**long** **longest**
4. Todd is _____, but Bob is the _____.	**strong** **strongest**
5. You may be _____ than me, but he is the _____.	**funnier** **funniest**
6. Yesterday was _____. Today is even _____.	**colder** **cold**
7. This pig is _____. That pig is the _____ of all.	**fat** **fattest**
8. She can swing _____, but I can swing _____.	**higher** **high**

Verbs

Name_____ Date_____

Verbs are words that show action and tell what is happening.

The girl **reads** a book.

Circle the verb in each sentence.

1. The motorcycles race down the street.

2. The boy throws the ball to the catcher.

3. The ducks swim quickly in the pond.

4. My dog always begs for food at the table.

5. Dad listens to the game on the radio.

6. The teacher writes our lesson on the board.

7. Leaves fall from the trees in autumn.

8. The little red hen works in her garden.

9. The little baby sleeps in a crib.

10. Birds fly south during the winter months.

Verbs in Agreement

Name_____ Date_____

Sometimes **s** is added to a verb when one person or thing is doing the action. When more than one person or thing is doing the action, there is no **s** added to the verb.

The boy kick**s** the ball.   The boy**s** play catch.

Circle the word that completes each sentence. Write it on the line.

1. The girls _____ to the library.	**walk**	**walks**
2. Boats _____ across the lake.	**sail**	**sails**
3. My dog _____ the squirrel.	**chase**	**chases**
4. She _____ to sew her own clothes.	**like**	**likes**
5. Six birds _____ on the telephone wire.	**sit**	**sits**
6. The worker _____ the club house.	**build**	**builds**
7. Julie _____ Mom wash the dishes.	**help**	**helps**
8. We _____ dinner at 6:00.	**eat**	**eats**

Verbs: Past Tense (1)

Name_____ Date_____

Add **ed** to most verbs to show the action took place in the past. call → call**ed**

For verbs that end in a silent **e**, just add **d**. use → use**d**

When a verb ends in **y**, change the **y** to **i** and add **ed**. cry → cr**ied**

Rewrite each verb to show the past tense.

1. help _____

2. wish _____

3. save _____

4. bake _____

5. plant _____

6. hurry _____

7. roll _____

8. fry _____

9. twirl _____

10. carry _____

11. walk _____

12. want _____

13. like _____

14. move _____

15. work _____

16. laugh _____

Name_____ Date_____

Rewrite each verb to tell about the past.

1. The circus bears _____.
   dance

2. The team _____ they would win the championship.
   hope

3. My Uncle got _____ last weekend.
   marry

4. The girls _____ TV all night.
   watch

5. Dad _____ his new car.
   wash

6. The chipmunk _____ to the top of the tree.
   climb

7. I _____ my last pencil.
   sharpen

8. He _____ here last year.
   move

Verbs with -ing (I)

Name_____ Date_____

To make some verbs tell about an action happening now,
add **ing** to the end of the verb.   look → look**ing**

When a verb ends in a silent **e**, drop the e and add **ing**.   bake → bak**ing**

Rewrite each verb with **ing**.

1. pass _____

2. joke _____

3. jump _____

4. rain _____

5. wait _____

6. use _____

7. clean _____

8. save _____

9. stay _____

10. mix _____

11. hope _____

12. help _____

13. move _____

14. stare _____

15. chew _____

16. show _____

Unit 3

Verbs with -ing (II)

Name_____ Date_____

Rewrite each verb to tell about now.

1. I am _____ my sister with her homework.
   help

2. We are _____ the night at a friend's house.
   spend

3. She is _____ for her lost ring.
   look

4. Dad is _____ the car over there.
   park

5. Grandma is _____ a peach pie.
   bake

6. Our town is _____ plastic and glass.
   recycle

7. The boy is _____ his new bike.
   ride

8. Who are you _____ on the phone?
   talk

Verbs in Context (1)

Name_____ Date_____

Circle the verb that completes each sentence. Write it on the line.

Unit 3

1. Yesterday, John _____ with his friend.	**plays** **played** **playing**
2. Beavers _____ at the wood.	**gnaw** **gnaws** **gnawing**
3. The crowd _____ for the home team.	**cheer** **cheers** **cheering**
4. Jeff is _____ to get to work on time.	**rush** **rushes** **rushing**
5. The ants _____ in a straight line.	**march** **marches** **marching**
6. Our class is _____ a story.	**read** **reads** **reading**
7. Do you hear the baby _____?	**cries** **cried** **crying**
8. The man _____ he would be chosen.	**hope** **hoped** **hoping**

Verbs in Context (II)

Name_____ Date_____

Circle the verb in each sentence. If it is not used correctly, rewrite the correct verb on the line.

1. The horse gallop through the forest. _____

2. Last night, we walking to the store. _____

3. Mom is clean the kitchen floor. _____

4. The frog sits on the lily pad. _____

5. Please writing your name in pencil. _____

6. Yesterday, the scouts roasted marshmallows. _____

7. The class is learned about government. _____

8. A strong man lift the heavy crate. _____

9. I will color the hippo pink. _____

10. We wait two hours for mom to come home. _____

Name_____ Date_____

Circle all the verbs.

1. couch   turn   call   jump   magic   point   ball   rope

2. whistle   turtle   skate   book   chair   box   paint   truck

---

Fill in the circle next to the correct verb.

3. Why did he _____ the window?   ○ a) close   ○ b) closed

4. My kitten _____ when she is happy.   ○ a) purring   ○ b) purrs

5. The boy _____ when he fell off his bike.   ○ a) cry   ○ b) cried

6. The big lion _____ at the crowd   ○ a) roars   ○ b) roaring

7. I like to _____ with my little brother.   ○ a) wrestle   ○ b) wrestled

8. Mom _____ at the funny show.   ○ a) laughs   ○ b) laughing

9. Dad _____ my room purple.   ○ a) painting   ○ b) painted

10. Please _____ off the lights.   ○ a) turned   ○ b) turn

Irregular Verbs

Name_____ Date_____

Some verbs change in special ways to tell about the past.

Now	In the Past
come, comes	came
say, says	said
sit, sits	sat
write, writes	wrote
run, runs	ran
see, sees	saw

Circle the word that completes each sentence. Write it on the line.

1. Let's _____ to the top of the hill.   **run**   **ran**

2. I _____ my name with a crayon.   **writes**   **wrote**

3. Mom _____ it is time to come home.   **say**   **said**

4. Did you _____ the monkey swing?   **see**   **saw**

5. Grandpa _____ to visit us last week.   **come**   **came**

6. Can you _____ to the swim party?   **come**   **came**

7. She will _____ a letter to her pen pal.   **write**   **wrote**

8. We _____ by the fire on the cold winter night.   **sits**   **sat**

Verb Usage: am, are, and is (1)

Name_____ Date_____

Sometimes, verbs also tell what someone or something is. We use three words to tell what someone or something is: **am**, **are**, and **is**.

Verb Chart	
I	am
You	are
He, She, or It	is
We	are
They	are

Write **am**, **are**, or **is** to complete each sentence.

1. Leaves _____ green.

2. Nan _____ a girl.

3. We _____ friends

4. He _____ a great goalie!

5. I _____ not feeling well.

6. The dogs _____ barking.

7. Kyle _____ not here today.

8. _____ it time to eat?

9. I _____ smart.

10. This peach _____ sweet.

11. You _____ happy.

12. They _____ not coming.

13. _____ you tired?

14. She _____ playing a game.

15. We _____ leaving now.

16. The flowers _____ pretty.

Verb Usage: am, are, and is (II)

Name_____ Date_____

Circle the verb in each sentence. If it is not used correctly, rewrite the correct verb on the line.

1. Tim and Tom is twins. _____

2. The elephants are smelly. _____

3. You is late for school! _____

4. They am going on a trip. _____

5. I am having a hot dog for lunch. _____

6. Our neighbors is moving to Ohio. _____

7. It is a cloudy day. _____

8. Are you having a bad day? _____

9. We is looking for Mom's watch. _____

10. The wind are blowing hard. _____

Verb Usage: does and do

Name_____ Date_____

The verbs **does** and **do** are special. Use **does** after the words **he**, **she**, and **it**, or with a noun. Use **do** after the words **I**, **you**, **we**, and **they**, or with a plural noun.

does	do
he, she, it	I, you, we, they
noun	plural noun

Write **does** or **do** or complete each sentence.

1. It _____ look like a good day for a picnic.

2. Most people _____ their best.

3. She _____ good tricks.

4. Sharks _____ swim very fast.

5. I _____ my homework.

6. _____ you like to read?

7. Jason _____ his chores.

8. The worker _____ a good job.

9. _____ the robot work?

10. He _____ not like to play video games.

Unit 3

Verb Usage: has and have (I)

Name_____ Date_____

The verbs **has** and **have** are special. Use **has** after the words **he**, **she**, and **it**, or with a noun. Use **have** after the words **I**, **you**, **we**, and **they**, or with a plural noun.

has	have
he, she, it noun	I, you, we, they plural noun

Write **has** or **have** to complete each sentence.

1. She _____ a new kitten.

2. Squirrels _____ long, bushy tails.

3. Do you _____ the time?

4. The baby _____ a high fever.

5. It _____ black and white stripes.

6. Paul _____ a great card collection.

7. The city _____ a statue downtown.

8. He _____ to stay after school.

9. The birds _____ a clean birdbath.

Verb Usage: has and have (II)

Name_____ Date_____

Unit 3

Circle the verb in each sentence. If it is not used correctly, rewrite the correct verb on the line.

1. The desert have a lot of mountains. _____

2. Billy have eaten too much candy. _____

3. It has begun to snow. _____

4. The players has worked very hard. _____

5. You has a nice jacket. _____

6. They has twelve chicken on their farm. _____

7. She has a spelling test tomorrow. _____

8. The boys have a great time playing together. _____

9. Has you ever been to Los Angeles? _____

10. An octopus has eight legs. _____

Name_____ Date_____

Some verbs change in special ways to tell about the past. See how **is**, **are**, and **am** change.

Now	In the Past
I **am**	I **was**
you **are**	you **were**
he, she, or it **is**	he, she, or it **was**
we **are**	we **were**
they **are**	they **were**

Write **was** or **were** to complete each sentence.

1. I _____ up in the tree.

2. Jason and David _____ going to the hockey game.

3. We _____ cooking over the campfire.

4. They _____ in the park.

5. Cindy _____ in the school play.

6. She _____ shivering in the cold outside.

7. You _____ on the phone.

8. The bus _____ late this morning.

9. That _____ an awesome ride!

Name_____ Date_____

Circle the verb in each sentence. If it is not used correctly, rewrite the correct verb on the line.

1. Where was you last night? _____

2. Sara was playing the piano. _____

3. Kelly and Frank was watching a movie. _____

4. They was planting trees in the park. _____

5. Were they coming for dinner? _____

6. The airplane were flying very low. _____

7. There were a bug crawling up my leg. _____

8. I was picking strawberries for Mom. _____

9. We were planning a surprise party for her. _____

10. Aunt Sue were baking cookies. _____

Unit 3

Verb Usage: saw and seen

Name_____ Date_____

Saw and **seen** are special forms of the verb **see**. Both tell about the past.

Use **saw** alone.
Use **seen** with **has** or **have**.

We **saw** a ladybug.
She **has seen** a ladybug.

Write **see** or **seen** to complete each sentence.

1. He has _____ a dolphin in the ocean.

2. They have _____ that show before.

3. My friend has _____ a shooting star.

4. Robert _____ his brother last week.

5. My family has never _____ the Rocky Mountains.

6. The girls _____ a funny clown.

7. The dog _____ the squirrel run up the tree.

8. Have you _____ the latest spring fashion show?

9. Mary _____ the lightening strike the house.

10. People have _____ many amazing things.

Verb Usage: did and had

Some verbs change in special ways to tell about the past.

Now	In the Past
has, have	had
does, do	did

Circle the verb that completes each sentence. Write it on the line.

1. Yesterday I _____ a fever.

   Today I _____ a cough.

   have

   had

2. Today farmers _____ hard jobs.

   Long ago, farmers _____ even harder jobs.

   do

   did

3. Yesterday Waldo _____ a silly trick.

   Now he _____ a better trick.

   did

   does

4. Yesterday Misty _____ no kittens.

   Now Misty _____ three kittens

   has

   had

5. Last week, Mom _____ a car accident.

   Now she _____ to get the car fixed.

   has

   had

6. The circus _____ arrive in town yesterday.

   We watched the clowns _____ their acts.

   do

   did

Unit 3

Verbs in Context (III)

Name_____ Date_____

Circle the verb in each sentence. If it is not used correctly, rewrite the correct verb on the line.

1. We have saw the parade last week.   _____

2. He do like to eat tomatoes.   _____

3. They were feeding the birds at the park.   _____

4. Yesterday, Kim do her homework.   _____

5. I am taller than my Mom!   _____

6. She has saved twenty dollars.   _____

7. We has a new girl in our class.   _____

8. It are fun to play basketball.   _____

9. They is the best neighbors.   _____

10. The boys are best friends.   _____

Adverbs (I)

Name_____ Date_____

Adverbs tell how an action is done. They answer the question "How?" and often end in **ly**.

Henry petted the goat gent**ly**.

Circle the adverb in each sentence.

1. The fire engine blew its horn loudly.

2. In the library, we talked quietly.

3. The old man walked slowly.

4. The girls giggled noisily.

5. The animals fought fiercely over the meat.

6. The sun shines brightly in my eyes.

7. The doctor wrapped the broken arm carefully.

8. The marine served his country proudly.

9. Race horses run quickly around the track.

10. Wind blew rapidly across the city.

Adverbs (II)

Adverbs tell how an action is done. Many **adverbs** are formed by adding **ly** at the end of an **adjective**.

nice + **ly** = nicely

She sang nicely.

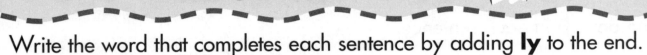

Write the word that completes each sentence by adding **ly** to the end.

bad	loud	peaceful	polite
silent	soft	slow	smooth	quick

1. The bunny hopped _____.

2. Fans cheered _____ for the winning team.

3. He _____ asked for a piece of cake.

4. The snail moved _____ across the sand.

5. When the band performed _____, everyone left.

6. The plane glided _____ through the sky.

7. The baby slept _____ through the storm.

8. The students read their books _____.

9. The kitten purred _____.

Name_____ Date_____

Fill in the circle next to each sentence that is written correctly.

1. ○ a) The bears are sleeping in the cave.
   ○ b) The bears is sleeping in the cave.

2. ○ a) She saw an old friend.
   ○ b) She have saw an old friend.

3. ○ a) Chad were late for dinner.
   ○ b) Chad was late for dinner.

4. ○ a) Yesterday, we had a picnic.
   ○ b) Yesterday, we has a picnic.

5. ○ a) The students does good work.
   ○ b) The students do good work.

6. ○ a) They is going on vacation.
   ○ b) They are going on vacation.

7. ○ a) The skateboarder does good tricks.
   ○ b) The skateboarder do good tricks.

8. ○ a) That man has a crooked cane.
   ○ b) That man have a crooked cane.

9. ○ a) We is going to the party.
   ○ b) We are going to the party.

10. ○ a) The wagon wheel was broken.
    ○ b) The wagon wheel were broken.

11. ○ a) Have you saw the new neighbors?
    ○ b) Have you seen the new neighbors?

12. ○ a) I am very tired today.
    ○ b) I is very tired today.

13. ○ a) Last night, we had pizza.
    ○ b) Last night, we has pizza.

14. ○ a) The girl do her homework.
    ○ b) The girl does her homework.

Name_____ Date_____

Put the following words in order to make a complete sentence.
Write the sentence on the line.

1. is to hot going Dad cook dogs

   _____

2. her book found lost Julie

   _____

3. every my I day pet hamster feed

   _____

4. the in was line first Tom one

   _____

5. the in played the mud pig

   _____

6. ice boy on the slipped the

   _____

7. fly wish I a like I could bird

   _____

8. the farmer's we market visited

   _____

Subjects (1)

The **subject** of a sentence tells who or what is doing the action.

<u>The elf</u> dances a jig.

~~~~~~

Underline the subject in each sentence.

1. A bud blossomed into a beautiful flower.

2. Matthew kicked the winning field goal.

3. The second grade class did a science experiment.

4. A tiny ant built a large sand hill.

5. I helped Grandma do the grocery shopping.

6. The clock on the wall is broken.

7. Seven goldfish swam happily in the aquarium.

8. The little girl hugged her pink teddy bear.

9. A wicked witch brewed up a special potion.

Unit 4

Name_____ Date_____

Match each subject with the best action to complete the sentence.
Write the letter on the line.

1. The magician ____   a) splashed in the icy water.

2. A shiny quarter ____   b) let us stay up late.

3. The boy's new skateboard ____   c) pulled a bird from his hat.

4. Penguins ____   d) are now extinct.

5. The army general ____   e) blasted to the moon.

6. Our baby sitter ____   f) rolled under my bed.

7. The space shuttle ____   g) lost a wheel.

8. Triceratops ____   h) gave orders to the men.

Write your own subject for each sentence.

9. _____ took a trip to Florida.

10. _____ answered the phone.

Compound Subjects

Name_____ Date_____

When two sentences have different subjects but the same action, the sentences can be combined into one by adding **and** between the subjects. The new subject is called a **compound subject**.

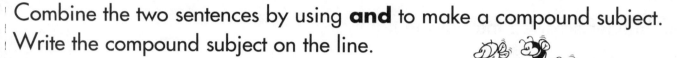

Frogs hop. Toads hop.
Frogs **and** toads hop.

Combine the two sentences by using **and** to make a compound subject. Write the compound subject on the line.

1. Flies buzz. Bees buzz.

_____ buzz.

2. Dogs run. Cats run.

_____ run.

3. Girls play soccer. Boys play soccer.

_____ play soccer.

4. Rain ruined the picnic. Wind ruined the picnic.

_____ ruined the picnic.

5. Lisa painted a picture. Robby painted a picture.

_____ painted a picture.

6. Mom washed the dishes. I washed the dishes.

_____ washed the dishes.

Name_____ Date_____

The **predicate** of a sentence
is the action that the subject is doing.

Many cars <u>race around the track</u>.

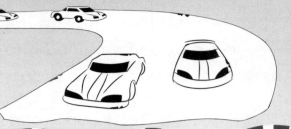

Underline the predicate in each sentence.

1. The builder screwed the bolts in tightly.

2. Thunder and lightening shook the sky.

3. Jason won the spelling bee.

4. Hot lava erupted form the volcano.

5. My brother broke Mom's favorite vase.

6. In gym class, we played kickball.

7. Mrs. Jones drove us to school this morning.

8. Workers changed the flat tire.

9. The doorbell rang.

Name_____ Date_____

Write a predicate from the box to complete each sentence.

eats a good breakfast	claps his hands
chose a good book	live in a castle
blew the man's hat	rode a camel
packed his suitcase for the trip	watered the garden

1. At the children's zoo, we _____.

2. The strong wind _____.

3. Hannah _____.

4. The king and queen _____.

5. Our librarian _____.

6. The lady _____.

7. Dad _____.

8. The baby _____.

Compound Predicates

Name_____ Date_____

When two sentences have the same subject but different actions, the sentences can be combined into one by adding **and** between the predicates. The new predicate is called a **compound predicate**.

Derek <u>ran</u>. Derek <u>swam</u>.
Derek <u>ran</u> **and** <u>swam</u>.

Combine the two sentences by using **and** to make a compound predicate. Write the compound predicate on the line.

1. Mary coughs. Mary sneezes.

   Mary _____.

2. My dog barks. My dog begs.

   My dog _____.

3. The glass fell. The glass broke.

   The glass _____.

4. The giant shouts. The giant roars.

   The giant _____.

5. The band plays. The band marches.

   The band _____.

6. Leaves change color. Leaves fall.

   Leaves _____.

Name_____ Date_____

Draw one line under the subject and two lines under the predicate in each sentence.

1. We skated on the frozen pond.

2. Jake and Todd play a card game.

3. The little girl dreamed about a magical fairy.

4. Snails and turtles move slowly.

5. The acrobats and the clowns performed perfectly.

6. The explorers discovered a new island.

7. Grandma baked a cake and a pie.

8. A hungry caterpillar ate through a leaf.

9. The rainstorm destroyed the roof on the house.

10. People listened to the orchestra music.

Unit 4

Invitations

Imagine you could invite anyone to lunch. Whom would you invite?

Fill in this invitation. Write these things:
Line 1: today's date
Line 2: the name of the person you are inviting
Lines 3-4: what you're inviting the person to
Lines 5-7: the day, time, and place of the event
Line 8: your own name

(1) _____ , **200** ____

(2) Dear _____ ,

(3) _____

(4) _____

(5) Day: _____

(6) Time: _____

(7) Place: _____

Your friend,

(8) _____

Thank You Letters

Name_____ Date_____

Look at the names of the different parts of a thank you letter.

Fill in this thank you letter. Write these things:
Line 1: today's date
Line 2: the name of the person you are thanking
Lines 3-5: what you're thanking the person for
Lines 6: your own name

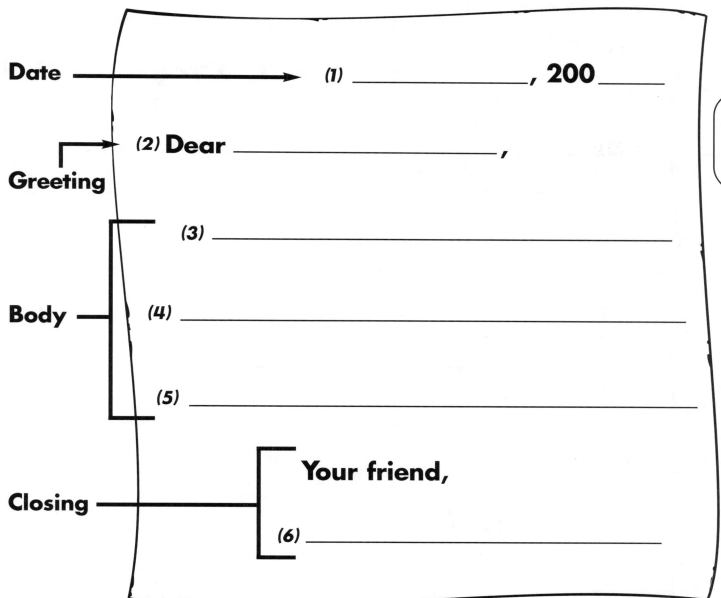

Date ⟶ (1) _____, **200**_____

Greeting ⟶ (2) **Dear** _____,

Body ⟶ (3) _____

(4) _____

(5) _____

Closing ⟶ **Your friend,**

(6) _____

Unit 4

Name_____ Date_____

Read the letter to answer the questions. Circle the answers.

1. Who wrote the letter?
   Linda   Ally

2. Who got the letter?
   Ally   Linda

3. What did it tell about?
   Linda   going to the zoo

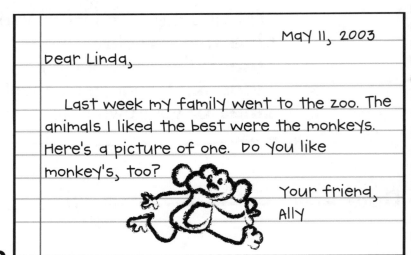

May 11, 2003

Dear Linda,

Last week my family went to the zoo. The animals I liked the best were the monkeys. Here's a picture of one. Do you like monkey's, too?

Your friend,
Ally

Write your own letter to a friend.

_____, 200___

Dear _____,

_____

_____

_____

Your friend,

_____

Compound Words (I)

Name_____ Date_____

A compound word is made of two smaller words.

dog　　+　　

house　　=　　

doghouse

Write a word from the box to finish each compound word below.
Then write the compound word.

boat	brush	fire	hair	lace	road	sand	scare

1. sail + _____ = _____

2. shoe + _____ = _____

3. camp + _____ = _____

4. _____ + cut = _____

5. _____ + box = _____

6. _____ + crow = _____

7. rail + _____ = _____

8. tooth + _____ = _____

Unit 5

Name_____ Date_____

Write a compound word to complete each sentence.

| doghouse | fireplace | flashlight | mailbox | seashells |
| skateboard | snowflakes | strawberry | sunburn | sunshine |

1. When the power goes out, we use our _____.

2. Tommy bought a new _____ ramp.

3. Mom got a bad _____ from laying in the sun.

4. Bruno's _____ is too small for him.

5. I like _____ jam on my toast.

6. The artist created a painting of _____ and starfish.

7. Our _____ keeps us warm in the cold winter.

8. Will there be _____ today or rain?

9. Put this letter in the _____.

10. The girls catch _____ on their tongues.

Contractions (I)

A **contraction** is two words put together. One or more letters are left out. In their place is this mark ' called an **apostrophe**.

apostrophe

she will = she + ~~will~~ = she'll
She'll eat vegetables anytime!

Match each pair of words with its contraction. Write the letter on the line.

1. I am ____   a) can't

2. she is ____   b) she's

3. we would ____   c) won't

4. they will ____   d) I'm

5. can not ____   e) doesn't

6. does not ____   f) we'll

7. you are ____   g) we'd

8. will not ____   h) don't

9. do not ____   i) they'll

10. we will ____   j) you're

Unit 5

Contractions (II)

Name_____ Date_____

Write the contraction that means the same as each pair of words.

couldn't didn't he's I'll isn't they've we're you're

1. he is _____

2. we are _____

3. I will _____

4. could not _____

5. they have _____

6. is not _____

7. you are _____

8. did not _____

Write the pair of words for each underlined contraction.

9. <u>We're</u> having a party. _____

10. <u>Let's</u> play a game. _____

11. <u>They're</u> all having a good time. _____

12. <u>Aren't</u> you glad you came? _____

Compound and Contraction Practice

Name_____ Date_____

Write compound words by putting two words from the box together.

birth	brush	butter	crow	day	fly
man	paint	scare	snow	some	thing

1. _____

2. _____

3. _____

4. _____

5. _____

6. _____

Fill in the circle next to the correct contraction.

7. **were not**	○ a) won't	○ b) wouldn't	○ c) we'll	○ d) weren't
8. **did not**	○ a) don't	○ b) didn't	○ c) doesn't	○ d) didt'n
9. **we have**	○ a) we've	○ b) we'll	○ c) won't	○ d) weren't
10. **let us**	○ a) lets	○ b) let's	○ c) lettuce	○ d) lets'
11. **have not**	○ a) hadn't	○ b) who'd	○ c) havn't	○ d) haven't
12. **she will**	○ a) shell	○ b) she'll	○ c) she'd	○ d) she'l

Synonyms (I)

Name_____ Date_____

Synonyms are words that have the same or almost the same meaning.

Write a synonym from the box for each word.

angry bucket car close glad home jump large make
present quick raise rock sick sleep small story yell

1. happy _____

2. ill _____

3. big _____

4. build _____

5. fast _____

6. little _____

7. shut _____

8. tale _____

9. shout _____

10. nap _____

11. mad _____

12. gift _____

13. pail _____

14. house _____

15. auto _____

16. leap _____

17. lift _____

18. stone _____

Name_____ Date_____

Circle the synonym for the underlined word in each sentence.

1. The <u>noise</u> of the fire crackers echoed.	**yell**	**sound**
2. That <u>fast</u> horse won the race.	**quick**	**fat**
3. A funny clown made us <u>laugh</u>.	**giggle**	**cry**
4. We saw a <u>little</u> ant making a hill.	**thin**	**tiny**
5. My best <u>friend</u> is moving to Mississippi.	**pal**	**mother**
6. The <u>kind</u> boy helped the old lady with her bags.	**mad**	**nice**
7. The movie is about to <u>begin</u>.	**close**	**start**
8. The ball went <u>over</u> the player's head.	**above**	**across**
9. What do you <u>wish</u> for?	**good**	**hope**
10. Synonyms are very <u>simple</u> to learn.	**easy**	**hard**

Unit 5

Name_____ Date_____

Antonyms are words that have opposite or almost opposite meanings.

Write an antonym from the box for each word.

angry bucket car close glad home jump large make
present quick raise rock sick sleep small story yell

1. cold _____

2. short _____

3. sleep _____

4. empty _____

5. fast _____

6. black _____

7. up _____

8. dry _____

9. happy _____

10. first _____

11. new _____

12. narrow _____

13. start _____

14. soft _____

15. come _____

16. high _____

17. clean _____

18. poor _____

Name_____ Date_____

Circle the antonym for the underlined word in each sentence.

1. When can I <u>open</u> my gift?	**close** **give**
2. Lisa has <u>long</u> hair.	**short** **straight**
3. It is <u>cold</u> during winter.	**chilly** **hot**
4. My teacher is <u>sick</u> today.	**well** **happy**
5. The boy ate <u>many</u> pieces of candy.	**lots** **few**
6. We didn't see any stars at <u>night</u>.	**dark** **day**
7. Please do not <u>stand</u> on the furniture!	**sit** **walk**
8. The wrestler is very <u>weak</u>.	**ill** **strong**
9. The raft will not <u>sink</u> in the water.	**float** **drop**
10. Go to the <u>back</u> of the line.	**end** **front**

Unit 5

Homonyms (I)

Name_____ Date_____

Homonyms are words that sound alike, but do not have the same spelling or meaning. **Pear** and **pair** are **homonyms**.

pear  pair

Match each word with its homonym.

 1. **sun**   **rode**

 2. **meet**   **sale**

3. **road**   **son**

 4. **sail**   **tale**

5. **tail**   **meat**

 6. **see**   **tow**

 7. **ate**   **eight**

8. **toe**   **sea**

Homonyms (II)

Name_____ Date_____

Write the homonyms to complete each sentence.

1. The wind _____ the _____ blanket.	**blue** **blew**
2. Did you _____ the band over _____?	**hear** **here**
3. We read a _____ about a dog's purple _____.	**tale** **tail**
4. When will my _____?	**heal** **heel**
5. The _____ _____ our beds.	**made** **maid**
6. Ron _____ on a rocky _____.	**road** **rode**
7. Danny _____ _____ cookies!	**eight** **ate**
8. Oh _____! A _____ ran in front of the car!	**dear** **deer**
9. Did you _____ the deep blue _____?	**sea** **see**
10. I would like _____ balloons _____.	**two** **too**

Name_____ Date_____

Fill in the circle next to the word that is a **synonym** for the word in the box.

1. large
○ a) small
○ b) run
○ c) huge

2. glad
○ a) happy
○ b) sad
○ c) angry

3. leap
○ a) walk
○ b) jump
○ c) sleep

4. sound
○ a) bell
○ b) quiet
○ c) noise

5. shut
○ a) close
○ b) open
○ c) push

6. little
○ a) small
○ b) big
○ c) baby

7. kind
○ a) mad
○ b) first
○ c) nice

8. pal
○ a) pail
○ b) friend
○ c) enemy

Fill in the circle next to the word that is a **antonym** for the word in the box.

9. good
○ a) eat
○ b) bad
○ c) happy

10. hard
○ a) soft
○ b) rough
○ c) rock

11. short
○ a) tiny
○ b) long
○ c) thin

12. tall
○ a) big
○ b) hope
○ c) short

13. smile
○ a) sweet
○ b) nice
○ c) frown

14. wide
○ a) huge
○ b) fat
○ c) narrow

15. push
○ a) pull
○ b) pinch
○ c) jump

16. near
○ a) far
○ b) close
○ c) there

Fill in the circle next to the word that is a **homonym** for the word in the box.

17. made
○ a) make
○ b) man
○ c) maid

18. two
○ a) toad
○ b) town
○ c) to

19. pail
○ a) pale
○ b) pane
○ c) path

20. rode
○ a) rod
○ b) road
○ c) roach

21. blew
○ a) blow
○ b) blue
○ c) blind

22. sun
○ a) son
○ b) sell
○ c) sale

23. cent
○ a) circle
○ b) can't
○ c) sent

24. here
○ a) help
○ b) hear
○ c) where

Prefix: re-

Prefixes are word parts added to the beginning of root words. The prefix **re** means "again."

prefix   root word

re   **+**   **build**   **=**   **rebuild**

Rebuild means "build again."

Add **re** to the beginning of each root word to make a new word. Circle the meaning of the new word.

1. _____read   **read**   **read again**

2. _____make   **make again**   **make**

3. _____try   **try**   **try again**

4. _____play   **play again**   **play**

5. _____pack   **pack again**   **pack**

6. _____heat   **heat**   **heat again**

7. _____tie   **tie**   **tie again**

8. _____write   **write again**   **write**

Unit 5

Prefix: un-

Name_____ Date_____

The prefix **un** means "not."

prefix		root word		
un	**+**	**tied**	**=**	**untied**

Untied means "not tied."

Add **un** to the beginning of each root word to make a new word.
Circle the meaning of the new word.

1. _____happy **not happy** **happy**

2. _____dressed **not dressed** **dressed**

3. _____lucky **lucky** **not lucky**

4. _____locked **lock** **not locked**

5. _____ripe **ripe** **not ripe**

6. _____wrapped **not wrapped** **wrapped**

7. _____safe **not safe** **safe**

8. _____opened **opened** **not opened**

Suffix: -ful

Name_____ Date_____

A **suffix** is a word part added to the end of a root word.
The suffix **ful** means "full of."

root word   suffix
peace   +   **ful**   =   **peaceful**

Peaceful means "full of peace."

Draw a line to match each word with its meaning.

1. graceful   full of tears

2. useful   full of grace

3. tearful   full of play

4. playful   full of use

Add **ful** to the end of each underlined word. Write the new word.

5. I feel full of <u>joy</u>. I feel _____.

6. Thanks for your <u>help</u>. You are very _____.

7. Take good <u>care</u> of that. Be _____.

8. I <u>wonder</u> how you did that? It is _____.

Suffix: -less

Name_____ Date_____

The suffix **less** means "without."

root word   suffix
hair **+** **less** **=** **hairless**

Hairless means "without hair."

Underline the suffix in each of these words.

1. painless   hopeless   colorless   nameless

_____

Write one of the words above to match each meaning below.

2. _____   3. _____
    without hope   without a name

4. _____   5. _____
    without pain   without color

_____

Write a word with the suffix **less** to complete the sentence.

6. The cat is without a home.

It is _____.

Suffix: -ly

Name_____ Date_____

The suffix **ly** means "in this way."

root word   suffix
brave   **+**   **ly**   **=**   **bravely**

Bravely means "in a brave way."

Underline the suffix in each of these words.

1.   surely   roughly   brightly   sadly

_____

Write one of the words above to match each meaning below.

2._____   3._____
     in a bright way   in a sure way

4._____   5._____
     in a rough way   in a sad way

_____

Write a word with the suffix **ly** to complete the sentence.

6. The snail moves in a slow way.

It moves _____.

Unit 5

Prefix and Suffix Practice

Name_____ Date_____

Circle the words with **prefixes**.

1. rewrite   unhappy   safely   unsure   useless   lovely   redraw   redo

2. colorful   unwrap   unpack   recheck   peaceful   loaded   weekly   unafraid

Circle the words with **suffixes**.

3. untie   helpful   powerful   toothless   unusual   rewind   slowly   remake

4. likely   useful   reread   grateful   undone   neatly   retie   wordless

Write a word from the box to complete each sentence.

hopeful   neatly   repay   painless   unable   unopened

5. Do your work in a neat way. Do it _____.

6. I have to pay my bill again. I need to _____ the bill.

7. The box is not opened. It is _____.

8. I am full of hope. I am _____.

9. He can't be there. He is _____ to attend.

10. My loose tooth has no pain. It is _____.

Alphabetical Order (1)

Name_____ Date_____

a b c d e f g h i j k l m n
o p q r s t u v w x y z

Write each group of words in alphabetical order.

1. train   boat
   ride   plane

_____
_____
_____
_____

2. bench   shell
   waves   fun

_____
_____
_____
_____

3. poke   march
   chase   jump

_____
_____
_____
_____

4. Venus   Mars
   Saturn   Earth

_____
_____
_____
_____

5. paint   circus
   horse   acrobat

_____
_____
_____
_____

6. dark   night
   star   moon

_____
_____
_____
_____

7. teacher   pencil
   work   friends

_____
_____
_____
_____

8. lemonade   juice
   soda   milk

_____
_____
_____
_____

9. screw   nail
   bolt   hammer

_____
_____
_____
_____

Unit 5

Name_____ Date_____

A B C 1 2 3

Put each group of words in alphabetical order by numbering them 1 to 3.

1.
___ honk
___ dive
___ master

2.
___ seed
___ forget
___ inside

3.
___ launch
___ shack
___ computer

4.
___ town
___ window
___ zipper

5.
___ elk
___ major
___ asleep

6.
___ phone
___ vulture
___ doctor

7.
___ lawyer
___ onion
___ metal

8.
___ board
___ wild
___ claw

9.
___ icicle
___ amaze
___ brush

10.
___ fire
___ police
___ emergency

11.
___ number
___ sling
___ crane

12.
___ gear
___ yawn
___ mask

13.
___ robot
___ granola
___ circle

14.
___ hurricane
___ pancake
___ snooze

15.
___ rooster
___ deck
___ light

16.
___ napkin
___ timber
___ spider

17.
___ branch
___ wasp
___ free

18.
___ ship
___ tooth
___ plug

19.
___ drum
___ flip
___ trick

20.
___ ear
___ buzz
___ tube

21.
___ keyboard
___ karate
___ knee

22.
___ parade
___ princess
___ pepper

23.
___ butterfly
___ braid
___ block

24.
___ sausage
___ soldier
___ shave

Name_____ Date_____

Fill in the circle if the group of words are in alphabetical order.

1. rectangle sand grumpy ○	2. jungle model rewrite ○	3. clip business locker ○	4. thread vampire yacht ○	5. grave hairy igloo ○
6. meal olive slide ○	7. refresh demand bent ○	8. change math front ○	9. lump picture scarf ○	10. ankle believe east ○
11. freeze dial hamburger ○	12. bottle present volcano ○	13. doorway member quarter ○	14. habitat whale flood ○	15. grape journey key ○
16. trash carve feather ○	17. ivy menu nest ○	18. under whistle zero ○	19. astronaut city turtle ○	20. plane clam soft ○
21. crash careful complete ○	22. mail mermaid mouth ○	23. railway remade robe ○	24. drop duckling data ○	25. web wheat woodchuck ○

Unit 5

Name_____ Date_____

The sentences below tell a story, but they are all mixed up.
Number them from 1 to 5 in the correct order.

_____ Kevin rode away on his new bike.

_____ The little man ate the food and told Kevin to make a wish.

_____ One day Kevin met a hungry little man.

_____ Kevin wished for a new bike.

_____ Kevin gave the little man some food.

Name_____ Date_____

Read the story.

Once upon a time there was a squirrel named Nutter. He would play all day long. Nutter liked to run up and down the trees. He enjoyed laying in the warm sun and hiding in the tall grass. He especially had fun chattering with his friends.

Then one day it began to get chilly. All the other squirrels were busy gathering nuts and berries for the cold winter ahead. Nutter didn't like to work, so he kept playing. Suddenly it began to snow. Nutter found himself cold and hungry. "I should have done my work," he thought. "I'm so hungry!" Luckily Nutter's best friend Bushy invited him to stay with him. Bushy shared his warm nest and nuts with Nutter. Nutter was grateful to have such a great friend!

Read the sentences and number them from 1 to 6 to show the order in which they happened in the story.

_____ Suddenly it began to snow.

_____ He would play all day.

_____ Bushy shared his warm nest and nuts with Nutter.

_____ He especially had fun chattering with his friends.

_____ Nutter found himself cold and hungry.

_____ All the other squirrels were busy gathering nuts and berries.

Unit 6

Name_____ Date_____

Fill in the circle next to the sentence that tells what will happen next.

1. Five inches of snow fell during the night.
   - ○ a) The teacher took the class to the museum.
   - ○ b) There was no school the next day.

2. Joey hurt his leg when he fell off his bike.
   - ○ a) Mom took him to the doctor.
   - ○ b) He rode his bike to the store.

3. It started to rain.
   - ○ a) Eric put on his bathing suit.
   - ○ b) Eric got out his umbrella.

4. The bushes in the front yard have grown tall.
   - ○ a) Dad will water the bushes.
   - ○ b) Dad will trim the bushes.

5. Mike knocked the cookie jar off the shelf.
   - ○ a) The cookie jar broke.
   - ○ b) Mike ate the cookies.

6. The baby birds are hungry.
   - ○ a) The mother bird will teach them to fly.
   - ○ b) The mother bird will feed them.

7. Jill's hair was messy and long.
   - ○ a) She had her picture taken.
   - ○ b) She got a new hair cut.

8. Laura studied her spelling words.
   - ○ a) She did well on the spelling test.
   - ○ b) She got every word wrong on the spelling test.

Predicting Outcomes (II)

Name_____ Date_____

Read each story. Underline the sentence that tells what happened next.

1. It was a hot day. Melanie got her swimsuit. Then she put suntan lotion on. She grabbed her towel and went outside. She met her friend Barb at the corner. Together they walked down to the park.

What will happen next?

Melanie and Barb will have a picnic.
Melanie and Barb will go swimming.
Melanie and Barb will go shopping.

2. Grandma and Mom had been picking strawberries all morning. They came home and washed them carefully. Mom cut the strawberries, while Grandma mixed sugar and flour together. Then they put them in a pan.

What will happen next?

Grandma and Mom will eat the strawberries.
Grandma and Mom will throw the strawberries away.
Grandma and Mom will bake a strawberry pie.

3. Jerry was walking home from school. He heard his neighbor calling for her cat. The cat was lost. Jerry helped the old lady look around the yard. Suddenly, Jerry heard a faint "Meow" from the top of the tree. The tree was too tall for Jerry to climb.

What will happen next?

The old lady will climb the tree.
Jerry will call the fire department.
They will wait for the cat to jump.

Unit 6

Main Idea (I)

The **main idea** is what the story is mostly about.

Read each story. Underline the sentence that tells the main idea.

1. Our family loves to go to the movies. I always get a big box of popcorn. My little brother eats gummy bears. Dad and Mom like to sit in the front row. My little sister always talks too much during the show.

_____

2. There is so much to do at the campground. You can go swimming or ride in a paddleboat. There is a big playground too. You can also go on a hayride or go hiking on the trails. It is great to sit by the warm fire and roast marshmallows.

_____

3. Mom looked around the kitchen. She saw glasses sitting in the sink. Crumbs were all over the table. Something red had been spilled on the floor. Bread and peanut butter were left on the counter. The kitchen was a mess!

_____

4. I had a hard time waking up this morning. My alarm clock rang, my mom called me, and my dog jumped on my bed. Finally, I smelled breakfast cooking. I jumped up quickly and ran downstairs.

Name_____ Date_____

Read each story. Fill in the circle next to the sentence that tells the main idea.

1. Eddie walked into the toy store. There were toys everywhere! He saw trucks, cars and bikes. There were lots of action figures and games. He saw things to build and remote control airplanes. Eddie couldn't believe how many toys there were!

   ○ a) Eddie saw a lot of action figures and games.
   ○ b) The toy store was filled with toys.
   ○ c) Eddie bought a new toy.

2. Your body is full of bones. Some bones are little and some are big. Each bone is connected to another bone to make up your skeleton. Your skeleton gives you your shape and without it you would fall down like a stuffed animal.

   ○ a) Bones are connected to each other.
   ○ b) Some bones are big and some are little.
   ○ c) Your body is full of bones.

3. A camel can live for many days with little food or water to drink. Some people think the camel uses water stored in its hump for water. Actually, camels store fat in their humps, which allows them to survive without food. Camels do like to eat leaves, grass, oats, and plants that grow in the desert.

   ○ a) Camels can live for days with little food.
   ○ b) Camels live in the desert.
   ○ c) Camels store fat in their humps.

Unit 6

Details (1)

Name_____ Date_____

Details tell more about the main idea.

Look for details as you read this story.

Last night our family had a picnic in our yard. We ate hot dogs, cheese, and fruit. We played hide-and-seek. When it got dark, we went inside. I love picnics!

Write the answer to each question.

1. When did the family have a picnic?

_____

2. Where was the picnic?

_____

3. What did the family eat?

_____

4. What game did they play?

_____

5. What happened when it got dark?

_____

Name_____ Date_____

Read the story.

Dill was a big dinosaur that lived in a small cave. "I need a new cave," he cried. So one day he went out to search for a new cave. He found a nice large one in the deepest part of the forest. It was quiet and there were lots of yummy trees to nibble on.

But Dill was not happy. He felt lonely. All of his friends lived near his old cave. He decided he was going to search for another new cave closer to his friends. Two days later, Dill heard large footsteps in the forest. As he peeked out from his cave, he noticed a new family moving in next door. Now Dill would not be lonely.

Write the answer to each question.

1. Who was Dill?

_____

2. Where did he find a new cave?

_____

3. What was the forest like?

_____

4. Why was Dill sad?

_____

5. Who made the large footsteps?

_____

Unit 6

Name_____ Date_____

Read the story.

    Adam and Kevin are best friends. They are in the same class and both enjoy school. Adam loves reading and writing stories. Kevin likes studying science and math. Kevin likes to learn new things in computer class, while Adam would rather do an art project. They like their teacher because she is really nice. Both of the boys think lunch and recess is the best!

The diagram below can be used to show how Adam and Kevin are alike and different. Write the number for each phrase in the appropriate space on the diagram. Then compare the results.

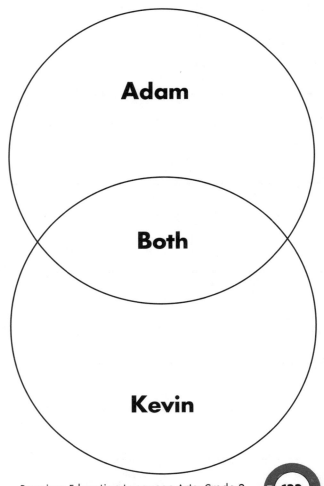

1. enjoys school
2. loves reading
3. likes lunch
4. likes math
5. studies science
6. learns new things on the computer
7. has a best friend
8. enjoys writing stories
9. thinks the teacher is nice
10. likes to do art projects

Drawing Conclusions

Name_____ Date_____

Read the stories. Fill in the circle next to the phrase that best completes each sentence.

The sun was just rising and Mom was working hard. She dug small holes. She sprinkled seeds into the holes and covered them with dirt. Then she watered the ground.

1. Mom was _____.
   ○ a) planting a garden
   ○ b) hiding a treasure

2. It was _____.
   ○ a) early in the morning
   ○ b) in the afternoon

Annie was staring out her window. It was dark and cloudy. Cars were splashing through puddles. People were walking around with umbrellas.

3. It was _____.
   ○ a) snowing outside
   ○ b) raining outside

4. Annie could not _____.
   ○ a) eat lunch
   ○ b) go out to play

The two girls had a lot of fun together. First they played on the seesaw. Then they pushed each other on the swings. The girls raced down the big slide and then plopped on the grass and giggled.

5. The two girls _____.
   ○ a) are best friends
   ○ b) don't know each other

6. They are _____.
   ○ a) at the zoo
   ○ b) at the park

Inferences (1)

Name_____ Date_____

Read each riddle. Circle the answer and write it on the line.

1. I am kept in a box.
   I come in lots of colors.
   I can help you draw a picture.
   What am I?

   _____

   scissors   a crayon   paper

2. You put me on your feet.
   I keep you warm and dry.
   I help you walk through the snow.
   What am I?

   _____

   boots   slippers   socks

3. I am played in the summer.
   Sometimes I get rained out.
   You use a bat and ball.
   What sport am I?

   _____

   soccer   golf   baseball

4. You can lick me.
   I get stuck on a lot of envelopes.
   You need me before you can mail
   a letter. What am I?

   _____

   a package   a stamp   a mailbox

5. I come in different shapes.
   I usually have a tail.
   I fly high on windy days.
   What am I?

   _____

   an airplane   a bird   a kite

6. I sometimes work in a hospital.
   Sometimes I work in an office.
   I help people who are sick.
   Who am I?

   _____

   a teacher   a doctor   a painter

Name_____ Date_____

Read each story. Circle the sentence that best describes what has happened. Then rewrite the sentence.

1. Mom looked through the cupboards. Then she made a list of things we needed. Next she went out. When she came home, we helped her unpack the bags. I put the milk in the refrigerator and Dad put the bread on the counter.

   Mom went to the grocery store.   **Mom is cleaning the kitchen.**

   _____

2. The man told everyone where to stand. He made sure he could see our whole family. Then he told us to say "cheese."

   The man took our food order.   **The man took our picture.**

   _____

3. The air is cooler. The leaves are beginning to turn colors. Squirrels are busy gathering nuts. It is time to start a new school year.

   It is New Year's Day.   **Fall is here.**

   _____

4. Ian was in the goal box. The score was tied 3 to 3. The other team was getting ready to kick the ball. He jumped up and caught the ball and saved the winning goal.

   Ian is playing soccer.   **Ian is playing hockey.**

   _____

Unit 6

Name_____ Date_____

Read the story.

One morning, Meg went with her Dad to the lumber store. They bought all different lengths of wood. They bought several bags of nails and a new saw.

When they got home, Dad began sawing the pieces of wood and hammering them together. Meg watched her Dad as he worked very carefully. When Dad was finished, he painted it pink. Finally it was done and Meg could play with her dolls.

Fill in the circle next to the correct answer.

1. Where did Meg and her Dad go?
   ○ a) to the playground   ○ b) to the lumber store   ○ c) to the grocery store

2. When they got home, what did Dad do first?
   ○ a) work carefully   ○ b) paint it pink   ○ c) saw the pieces of wood

3. Who painted it?
   ○ a) Meg   ○ b) Dad   ○ c) Meg and Dad

4. What did Dad build?
   ○ a) a doll house   ○ b) a swing set   ○ c) doghouse

5. A good title for this story would be _____.
   ○ a) Dad Buys Wood
   ○ b) Dad and Meg Work Together
   ○ c) Meg's New Doll House

Understanding Characters

Name_____ Date_____

Usually a story tells about a character. A **character** can be a person, animal, or several people or animals.

Read the story.

David had a birthday party. He gave each of his friends a big balloon. The children took their balloons outside. The wind began to blow. It was so strong it pulled the balloons up. The children held tight to their balloons. Suddenly, the balloon pulled David up…up…up. He was so surprised! It pulled his friends up in the air, too. Just then, some birds flew by and pecked holes in the balloons. All the children began to slowly float down to the ground. What a fun birthday party!

Circle the best answer(s) for each question.

1. Who is in the story?

David   David's mother   David's father   birds   David's friends

2. Who is the most important person in the story?

David   David's mother   David's best friend

3. Which words tell about David?

grown-up   young   sleepy   happy   sad

surprised   a girl   a crow   a boy

Unit 6

Cause and Effect (I)

Name_____ Date_____

A **cause** is the reason why something happens. An **effect** is what happens.

cause   effect

Because Paul overslept, | he was late for school.

Circle the best way to end each sentence.

1. Because Bill runs fast,

    he won the race.

    he is a good singer.

2. The puppy is sad

    because he lost his bone.

    because he is sleeping.

3. Because snow fell,

    the sun came out.

    Robin went sledding.

4. Mom is smiling

    because she has to wash clothes.

    because she got a nice gift.

5. Because it was raining,

    Lila is a good friend.

    Lila wore a raincoat.

6. The plant grew tall and strong

    because it is a tree.

    because Jenny gave it water.

7. The boy was in trouble

    because he played with his brother.

    because he called his brother a name.

8. Because the king is kind,

    many people like him.

    he likes ice cream.

Name_____ Date_____

Read the stories. Underline each sentence that tells why something happened.

1. A bear looked at the fish in the river. "What a fine lunch those fish would make!" he thought. The bear began to fish.

Why did the bear begin to fish?

He was thirsty.
He wanted fish for lunch.
He likes to fish.

2. Brian and Jordan were playing catch. One time, Jordan didn't catch the ball. The ball crashed through a window.

Why did the window break?

Jordan didn't catch the ball.
The window had a crack in it.
Brian didn't catch the ball.

3. Some people think a ladybug is good luck. They like to eat insects that could harm plants and vegetables. Farmers like ladybugs in the gardens.

Why do farmers like ladybugs?

They are pretty.
They bring good luck.
They eat harmful insects.

4. Cory studied his spelling words every night. He wanted to get a good grade on his test. The next morning, Cory took his test and thought he misspelled every word. When he got his paper back, he was very happy!

Why was Cory happy?

He was glad the test was over.
He got a good grade.
He likes to take tests.

Unit 6

Fact and Opinion (I)

Name_____ Date_____

A **fact** is something you can prove. An **opinion** is what you feel or believe. You cannot prove it.

fact
Spot has brown eyes.
opinion
Spot has kind eyes.

Circle the fact in each pair of sentences.

1. Jumping rope is easy to do.
   Jumping rope is good exercise.

2. Baseball is fun.
   A baseball team has nine players.

3. A rose is a flower.
   Roses are pretty.

4. Dogs are good pets.
   Dogs cannot climb trees.

5. Everyone likes ice cream.
   This store sells ice cream.

6. This cap costs five dollars.
   This cap looks good on me.

Name_____ Date_____

Decide if each sentence is a fact or an opinion.
Circle **F** for **fact** or **O** for **opinion**.

1. Gina has curly hair.   **F**   **O**

2. Turtles are ugly.   **F**   **O**

3. Summer is the best time of year.   **F**   **O**

4. The tree has smooth leaves.   **F**   **O**

5. Cats make the best pets.   **F**   **O**

6. The home team won the game.   **F**   **O**

7. Bats are the only mammals that can fly.   **F**   **O**

8. Reindeer live where it is very cold.   **F**   **O**

Unit 6

Name_____ Date_____

Read the story.

    Annie was sad. It was her birthday. But none of her friends had wished her a happy birthday all day.

    When she came home, she had a big surprise! All her friends were there. "Happy birthday, Annie!" they shouted. Annie felt happy then. Her friends wished her a happy birthday after all.

Fill in the circle next to the correct answer.

1. Who is this story about?
     ○ a) friends   ○ b) Mother   ○ c) Annie

2. Why was Annie sad?
     ○ a) None of her friends wished her a happy birthday.
     ○ b) She was having a party.
     ○ c) It was her birthday.

3. Where does this story take place?
     ○ a) at school   ○ b) at a restaurant   ○ c) at Annie's house

4. Is it a fact that Annie was happy at the end?
     ○ a) Yes   ○ b) No

Name_____ Date_____

Fill in the circle next to the word that has the same **vowel sound** as the first word in each row.

1. **pump**   ○ a) rude   ○ b) run   ○ c) gate   ○ d) then

2. **kite**   ○ a) hide   ○ b) mitt   ○ c) read   ○ d) luck

3. **noodle**   ○ a) copy   ○ b) book   ○ c) hut   ○ d) moose

4. **head**   ○ a) knee   ○ b) giant   ○ c) meadow   ○ d) leak

5. **haul**   ○ a) tumble   ○ b) oil   ○ c) draw   ○ d) take

6. **plow**   ○ a) house   ○ b) blow   ○ c) stop   ○ d) tune

7. **coil**   ○ a) royal   ○ b) cot   ○ c) bone   ○ d) rattle

8. **new**   ○ a) tumble   ○ b) bread   ○ c) grew   ○ d) puddle

9. **farm**   ○ a) your   ○ b) scarf   ○ c) bake   ○ d) bath

10. **third**   ○ a) sign   ○ b) torch   ○ c) caught   ○ d) dirt

11. **curl**   ○ a) part   ○ b) fern   ○ c) buckle   ○ d) team

12. **sport**   ○ a) thorn   ○ b) hole   ○ c) barn   ○ d) chop

Unit 7

Practice Test: Blends and Digraphs

Name_____ Date_____

Fill in the circle that has the same **beginning sound** as the first word in each row.

1. **blue**	○ a) bunny	○ b) blimp	○ c) plane	○ d) slip
2. **screw**	○ a) smoke	○ b) squirrel	○ c) scrub	○ d) stripe
3. **shade**	○ a) snake	○ b) ship	○ c) swish	○ d) sail
4. **what**	○ a) wheat	○ b) thump	○ c) shell	○ d) chip
5. **phone**	○ a) write	○ b) shine	○ c) find	○ d) pants
6. **nice**	○ a) snip	○ b) knit	○ c) think	○ d) lump

Fill in the circle that has the same **ending sound** as the first word in each row.

7. **bench**	○ a) teach	○ b) nickel	○ c) bent	○ d) cook
8. **list**	○ a) tent	○ b) test	○ c) miss	○ d) tick
9. **brush**	○ a) risk	○ b) shout	○ c) beach	○ d) trash
10. **ant**	○ a) tooth	○ b) band	○ c) went	○ d) pan
11. **thumb**	○ a) comb	○ b) tube	○ c) sink	○ d) junk

Name_____ Date_____

Read the sentences. Fill in the circle next to the part that is not written correctly.

1.
- ○ a) Has anyone seen my math
- ○ b) homework I thought I left it on
- ○ c) the table.

2.
- ○ a) Wow Did you see that?
- ○ b) The baseball player just
- ○ c) hit a grand slam.

3.
- ○ a) Last week our family went
- ○ b) to florida. We had a great
- ○ c) time visiting Grandma.

4.
- ○ a) tim is my best friend. We
- ○ b) like to play hide-and-seek
- ○ c) in the dark.

5.
- ○ a) My dog had puppies last
- ○ b) week. I hope Mom will let
- ○ c) me keep one

6.
- ○ a) Eat your vegetables Mom
- ○ b) tells us we will get strong
- ○ c) muscles and bones.

7.
- ○ a) I can't wait until Sunday.
- ○ b) I'm having a birthday party
- ○ c) with all my friends.

8.
- ○ a) I heard the fans cheering
- ○ b) loudly. Who won the game
- ○ c) The Racers won 7 to 6.

Unit 7

Name_____ Date_____

Fill in the circle next to the word that completes each sentence.

1. Grandma planted red _____ in her garden.
   ○ a) flower   ○ b) flowers   ○ c) floweres

2. I lost a new _____ on the bus.
   ○ a) necklace ○ b) necklaces ○ c) necklacies

3. Three _____ flew over the moon.
   ○ a) witch   ○ b) witchs   ○ c) witches

4. All the _____ had fun at the slumber party.
   ○ a) girl   ○ b) girls   ○ c) girl's

5. Cathy needs to wear _____ for reading.
   ○ a) glass   ○ b) glasss   ○ c) glasses

6. The lady gave me six _____ on my ice cream.
   ○ a) cherries ○ b) cherry   ○ c) cherrys

7. Those _____ need to be sent back to the store.
   ○ a) box   ○ b) boxes   ○ c) boxs

8. We rode in a _____ to the airport.
   ○ a) taxi   ○ b) taxis   ○ c) taxies

Practice Test: Pronouns and Adjectives

Name_____ Date_____

Fill in the circle next to the **pronoun** that could replace the underlined word(s).

1. Come with <u>Mary and me</u> to the skating rink.
   ○ a) they   ○ b) we   ○ c) us

2. <u>The horse</u> is galloping through the field.
   ○ a) It   ○ b) You   ○ c) Them

3. <u>The boy</u> walked home alone.
   ○ a) We   ○ b) He   ○ c) She

4. We will visit <u>Grandma and Grandpa</u> soon.
   ○ a) them   ○ b) us   ○ c) they

Fill in the circle next to the **adjective** that best completes each sentence.

5. The _____ crow sat on the scarecrow.
   ○ a) town   ○ b) smart   ○ c) black

6. Yesterday, we went to a _____ reunion.
   ○ a) hungry   ○ b) family   ○ c) wet

7. My cat had _____ kittens.
   ○ a) five   ○ b) easy   ○ c) dusty

8. The baby fell asleep on the _____ pillow.
   ○ a) bushy   ○ b) strong   ○ c) soft

Practice Test: Verbs

Name_____ Date_____

Fill in the circle next to the **verb** that best completes each sentence.

1. The football player ____ a field goal.
   ○ a) kick   ○ b) kicked   ○ c) kicking

2. A squirrel is ____ on an acorn.
   ○ a) chew   ○ b) chewed   ○ c) chewing

3. Mom and I ____ for a new coat.
   ○ a) shop   ○ b) shops   ○ c) shopping

4. Yesterday, we ____ a funny video.
   ○ a) watch   ○ b) watched   ○ c) watching

5. Dad ____ a job in a tall building.
   ○ a) has   ○ b) are   ○ c) have

6. The teacher ____ not give us homework.
   ○ a) is   ○ b) do   ○ c) did

7. The team ____ given a trophy for winning the championship.
   ○ a) were   ○ b) have   ○ c) was

8. Did you ____ my yellow earring?
   ○ a) seen   ○ b) see   ○ c) saw

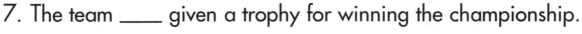

Practice Test: Subjects and Predicates

Name_____ Date _____

Fill in the circle next to the sentence in which the **subject** is underlined.

1. ○ a) The children <u>petted</u> goats at the zoo.
   ○ b) The children petted goats <u>at the zoo</u>.
   ○ c) <u>The children</u> petted goats at the zoo.

2. ○ a) <u>Snow</u> is falling on the tree tops.
   ○ b) <u>Snow is falling</u> on the tree tops.
   ○ c) Snow is falling <u>on the tree tops</u>.

3. ○ a) Zack and Nick <u>like to play the guitar</u>.
   ○ b) <u>Zack and Nick</u> like to play the guitar.
   ○ c) <u>Zack and Nick like to play</u> the guitar.

Fill in the circle next to the sentence in which the **predicate** is underlined.

4. ○ a) Mom spilled her coffee <u>on the rug</u>.
   ○ b) <u>Mom</u> spilled her coffee on the rug.
   ○ c) Mom <u>spilled her coffee on the rug</u>.

5. ○ a) <u>Sherry</u> sings and dances in the show.
   ○ b) Sherry <u>sings and dances in the show</u>.
   ○ c) <u>Sherry sings and dances</u> in the show.

6. ○ a) The puppy <u>wags his tail</u>.
   ○ b) <u>The puppy wags</u> his tail.
   ○ c) The puppy wags <u>his tail</u>.

Unit 7

Name_____ Date_____

Fill in the circle next to the word that is a **synonym** for the first word.

1. **kind**   ○ a) mean   ○ b) nice   ○ c) cute   ○ d) little

2. **trash**   ○ a) can   ○ b) rash   ○ c) garbage   ○ d) list

3. **shut**   ○ a) close   ○ b) open   ○ c) window   ○ d) move

4. **pretty**   ○ a) ugly   ○ b) girl   ○ c) happy   ○ d) beautiful

Fill in the circle next to the word that is an **antonym** for the first word.

5. **deep**   ○ a) hole   ○ b) shallow   ○ c) many   ○ d) big

6. **easy**   ○ a) hard   ○ b) soft   ○ c) look   ○ d) simple

7. **far**   ○ a) away   ○ b) drive   ○ c) near   ○ d) distant

8. **morning**   ○ a) day   ○ b) awake   ○ c) star   ○ d) night

Fill in the circle next to the word that is a **homonym** for the first word.

9. **road**   ○ a) ride   ○ b) run   ○ c) rode   ○ d) rows

10. **son**   ○ a) sun   ○ b) sell   ○ c) silk   ○ d) boy

11. **heel**   ○ a) haul   ○ b) help   ○ c) heal   ○ d) hello

12. **pail**   ○ a) bucket   ○ b) pale   ○ c) paint   ○ d) play

Practice Test: Prefixes and Suffixes

Name_____ Date_____

Fill in the circle next to the correct word.

1. to spell again ○ a) respell ○ b) unspell	**2. opposite of pack** ○ a) repack ○ b) unpack	**3. to make again** ○ a) remake ○ b) unmake
4. opposite of wrap ○ a) rewrap ○ b) unwrap	**5. opposite of safe** ○ a) resafe ○ b) unsafe	**6. to appear again** ○ a) reappear ○ b) unappear
7. without care ○ a) careful ○ b) careless	**8. in a happy way** ○ a) happiness ○ b) happily	**9. without hair** ○ a) hairless ○ b) hairy
10. full of hope ○ a) hopeful ○ b) hopeless	**11. full of play** ○ a) playful ○ b) playless	**12. without a home** ○ a) homely ○ b) homeless

Unit 7

Name_____ Date_____

Read the story.

Once upon a time, there was a little green snake that lived in the forest. He was very lonely because he had no friends. Everyone was afraid of him.

One day the snake asked a beetle, "Would you like to be my friend?"

"No way!" said the beetle. "You would slither on top of me!"

Then the snake asked an owl, "Would you be my friend?"

The owl said, "I can't be your friend, I live in the trees."

Finally, as the snake was hiding under a rock, he heard a hissing sound. He peeked out and said, "Would you be my friend?"

It was another snake! "Sure," he said.

Fill in the circle next to the best answer.

1. This story is mainly about _____.
   ○ a) an owl   ○ b) a beetle   ○ c) a snake

2. The snake was lonely because _____.
   ○ a) he was ugly   ○ b) he had no friends   ○ c) he lived in the forest

3. Who did the snake ask to be his friend first?
   ○ a) a beetle   ○ b) dog   ○ c) an owl

4. What was the snake hiding under?
   ○ a) leaves   ○ b) a rock   ○ c) a bush

5. Who said he would be the snake's friend?
   ○ a) a rat   ○ b) another snake   ○ c) a fish

Answer Key

Page 3
1. cat   2. rock   3. man   4. duck
5. gum   6. bat   7. sock   8. mug
9. sand 10. pig 11. ham 12. dog
13. pot 14. drum 15. pin 16. pan

Page 4
1. pie   2. jeep   3. rake
4. mule 5. leaf 6. bike
7. globe 8. cake 9. robe
10. tube 11. bee 12. team

Page 5
1. paint   6. mine
2. Try   7. goat
3. dice   8. juice
4. peach 9. toe
5. tray

Page 6
1. long   2. long   3. long
4. short 5. long 6. short
7. long 8. short 9. short
10. long 11. short 12. long
13. short 14. long 15. short
16. short 17. long 18. short
19. long 20. short 21. short
22. long 23. long 24. short

Page 7
1. goose   2. moon   3. roof
4. tools 5. spoon 6. boot
7. noon 8. moose 9. balloon
10. tooth 11. broom 12. igloo

Page 8
1. hook   6. wood
2. stood 7. good
3. book 8. Look
4. took 9. cookie
5. foot

Page 9
1. bread   2. spread   3. sweater
4. steak 5. head 6. feather
7. ready 8. heavy 9. weather
10. breakfast

Page 10
1. sweater 6. head
2. heavy 7. feathers
3. bread 8. healthy
4. leather 9. meadow
5. thread

Page 11
1. pause   6. launch
2. cause 7. haul
3. caught 8. taught
4. Paul 9. haunted
5. because 10. saucer

Page 12
1. naughty 6. August
2. autumn 7. caught
3. launch 8. pause
4. fault 9. haul
5. dinosaur

Page 13
1. straw 2. draw 3. crawl
4. yawn 5. hawk 6. saw
(Answers may vary for 7-12.)
7. raw, straw 8. dawn, fawn
9. jaws, laws 10. pawn, drawn
11. flaw, draw 12. bawl, shawl

Page 14
1. fawn   6. crawl
2. raw 7. saw
3. claws 8. paw
4. shawl 9. straw
5. drawing

Page 15
1. caught 6. jaw
2. spread 7. food
3. saw 8. took
4. breath 9. because
5. scoop

Page 16
1. c 4. d 7. a 10. c
2. b 5. a 8. b 11. b
3. a 6. b 9. d 12. c

Page 17
1. cloud 2. house 3. couch
4. hound 5. south 6. mouse
7. blouse 8. count 9. mouth
10. shout 11. sour 12. grouchy
13. found 14. out 15. pout

Page 18
1. loud   6. ground
2. Our 7. sprout
3. mouse 8. sound
4. bounce 9. found
5. pouch

Page 19
1. long o 2. (color) 3. (color)
4. long o 5. (color) 6. long o
7. (color) 8. long o 9. (color)
10. (color) 11. long o 12. (color)

Page 20
1. blow   6. know
2. town 7. show
3. tow 8. growl
4. How 9. plow
5. down

Page 21
1. foil   2. toy   3. coins
4. Roy 5. point 6. boy
7. join 8. enjoy 9. boil
10. noise

Answer Key

Page 22
1. boy, points
2. Roy, join
3. enjoys, toy
4. coins
5. moist, soil
6. choice
7. royal, broiled
8. noise, annoying
9. Joy, voice

Page 23
1. blew
2. flew
3. brew
4. knew
5. chew
6. few
7. grew
8. threw
9. drew

Page 24
1. new
2. few
3. Mew
4. news
5. knew
6. few
7. chew
8. stew
9. newspaper
10. blew
11. threw
12. screw
13. crew
14. grew
15. new

Page 25
1. loud
2. coin
3. blew
4. Our
5. bow
6. noise
7. owl
8. knew
9. crown

Page 26
1. joy
2. shout
3. grow
4. threw
5. south
6. frown
7. soy
8. new
9. our
10. shoe
11. toy
12. grew

Page 27
1. arm
2. park
3. star
4. mark
5. harp
6. party
7. card
8. yard
9. yarn
10. farm
11. car
12. jar

Page 28
1. charm
2. sharp
3. shark
4. harm
5. cart
6. dark
7. chart
8. far
9. smart

Page 29
1. bird
2. worm
3. turn
4. fern
5. earth
6. dirt
7. shirt
8. clerk
9. squirrel
10. stir
11. girl
12. nurse
13. germ, circus, firm, birthday
14. fur, turtle, hurt, skirt

Page 30
1. letter
2. thirty
3. batter
4. curl
5. skirt
6. twirl
7. squirts
8. hurt
9. dirt

Page 31
1. cork
2. orange
3. stork
4. horse
5. store
6. corn
7. fork
8. snore
9. horn
10. storm
11. forest
12. thorn

Page 32
1. fort
2. wore
3. porch
4. pork
5. sword
6. more
7. scored
8. chores
9. short

Page 33
1. river
2. first
3. fork
4. turtle
5. chirp
6. shark
7. farm
8. hard
9. nurse

Page 34
1. b
2. d
3. a
4. a
5. c
6. d
7. a
8. b
9. a
10. d
11. b
12. c

Page 35
1. plant
2. glove
3. block
4. brush
5. crab
6. crown
7. swim
8. spoon
9. snail
10. skate
11. frog
12. drip
13. clock
14. sled
15. crib
16. broom
17. star
18. tree
19. glue
20. flag

Page 36
1. spray
2. squirrel
3. straw
4. screw
5. string
6. spring
7. strong
8. scrub
9. strong
10. screw
11. spring
12. squirrel

Page 37
1. desk
2. wing
3. tent
4. hand
5. ring
6. wand
7. fist
8. truck
9. king
10. sand
11. sing
12. band
13. plant
14. swing
15. chick
16. skunk

Page 38
1. flute
2. flag
3. bridge
4. raft
5. skunk
6. bank
7. prince
8. squeeze
9. smoke

Page 39
1. pr
2. gl
3. fr
4. cl
5. dr
6. dr
7. nk
8. mp
9. sm
10. br
11. gl
12. tr
13. sk
14. st
15. str
16. sl
17. sl
18. lk
19. scr
20. sn
21. st
22. lamp
23. tent
24. clown
25. stop

Page 40
1. ch
2. sh
3. ch
4. ch
5. ch
6. ch
7. sh
8. sh
9. ch
10. sh
11. sh
12. ch
13. sh
14. sh
15. ch, ch
16. sh
17. ch
18. sh
19. ch
20. sh

Page 41
1. th
2. wh
3. th
4. wh
5. th
6. th
7. th
8. w
9. white
10. think
11. which
12. thorn

Answer Key

Page 42
1. alphabet
2. elephant
3. pheasant
4. photo
5. trophy
6. gopher
7. phonics
8. phantom
9. phony
10. Philadelphia
11. pharmacy
12. photographer

Page 43
1. cough
4. high
7. laugh
2. light
5. right
8. rough
3. thought
6. fight
9. through

Page 44
1. ch
2. ph
3. gh
4. ch
5. wh
6. ch
7. th
8. wh
9. ch
10. gh
11. ng
12. sh
13. wh
14. Th
15. wh
16. gh
17. Th
18. Ch
19. sh

Page 45
1. thumb
2. knock
3. wrist
4. knee
5. gnaw
6. write
7. knot
8. wring
9. wrap
10. lamb
11. wren
12. comb

Page 46
1. gnome
4. climb
7. write
2. wrong
5. wrench
8. knew
3. knight
6. crumb
9. knot

Page 47
1. c
2. b
3. b
4. a
5. c
6. a
7. d
8. c
9. gh
10. w
11. gh
12. gh
13. b
14. g
15. k
16. gh
17. g
18. gh
19. w
20. b
21. gh
22. k

Page 48
One, He, His, After, First,
Then, Next, Finally
1-2. (Sentences will vary.)

Page 49
Kate, I, Stinky, Stinky, Stinky,
Sniffer, Kate, I
1-2. (Sentences will vary.)

Page 50
Our class took a trip to the museum.
We saw all kinds of dinosaurs.
I felt like a mouse standing next to those huge models.
My favorite was the brontosaurus.
I wished I could've rode on its tail.
The teacher took our picture with a life-size raptor.
It was fun learning about the dinosaurs.
1-2. (Statements will vary.)

Page 51
1., 5., 7., 8., 11.

Page 52
2., 3., 4., 6., 9.

Page 53
"What do you think that was?" asked Josh.
"Do you think we should check it out?" Josh asked.
"What if there are aliens?" Tommy wondered.
"What would they look like? How would they speak? What if they took us into their spaceship?"
1-2. (Questions will vary.)

Page 54
1., 2., 5., 7., 10.

Page 55
I love going to amusement parks!
Woosh!
Look out!
I feel like I'm going to fly out of my seat!
Wow!
What a thrill!
1-2. (Exclamations will vary.)

Page 56
Zachary and his Grandpa went fishing. "Is this a good spot Grandpa?" asked Zachary.
"Perfect!" Grandpa said.
They began to cast their reels. Then Zachary noticed a sign. It read: No Fishing. Keep Out.
"Rats!" shouted Grandpa. "We'll have to go down the river a little farther," he said. Suddenly they came to the perfect spot. "Ahhh!" This is great!" cried Grandpa. "Do you need help baiting your hook?" he asked.
"No, I can do it," Zachary answered.
They cast their fishing lines into the water and waited. Grandpa told some stories while they ate a picnic lunch. Then Zachary felt something pulling on his line. "Oh, I think I got one!" he yelled. As he reeled in his line, the big fish tugged and tugged. "Help, Grandpa!" he screamed. Together they reeled in the big fish. But when Zachary looked, there was nothing on the end of the hook. "What happened?" he asked.
Grandpa replied, "That's the big one that got away."

Page 57
2., 3., 4., 5., 8., 9.

Answer Key

Page 58
1. frog, fly, tongue
2. Grandma, basket, cookies
3. David, game, computer
4. girl, bike, store
5. Mom, chicken, rice
6. kitten, yarn
7. truck, street
8. man, deck, days
9. Caterpillars, butterflies
10. doctor, lady, medicine

Page 59
1. Cherry Street
2. Chicago
3. Jeremy
4. Central School
5. Mr. Turner
6. Friday
7. Pacific Ocean
8. Memorial Day
9. December

Page 60
1. April
2. hay
3. giraffes
4. rocks
5. pool
6. Mrs. Smith
7. fish
8. rope
9. bananas
10. kangaroos
11. Rain Forest
12. plants
13. picnic
14. School
15. pictures

Page 61
1. bells
2. buses
3. trucks
4. kittens
5. boxes
6. peaches
7. eggs
8. lunches
9. boots
10. cups
11. dresses
12. dishes
13. pencils
14. girls
15. hats
16. wishes
17. mixes
18. trees

Page 62
1. candies
2. babies
3. ladies
4. cherries
5. puppies
6. flies
7. berries
8. daisies
9. cities
10. bunnies
11. berries
12. city
13. flies
14. lady
15. daisies

Page 63
1. coach's
2. dancers'
3. boy's
4. players'
5. teacher's
6. girl's
7. animals'
8. Dad's

Page 64
1. I
2. We
3. her
4. us
5. He
6. them
7. her

Page 65
1. I
2. him
3. They
4. She
5. me
6. us
7. them
8. We
9. them
10. me
11. us
12. She

Page 66
1. b
2. a
3. a
4. b
5. a
6. b
7. a
8. b
9. b
10. a
11. a
12. b
13. b
14. a
15. a
16. b
17. a
18. b
19. b
20. a

Page 67
1. red, green
2. One, tan
3. Nosy, old
4. gold, open
5. Three, happy
6. cool, blue
7. Shiny, green
8. Many, big

Page 68
1. fast, faster
2. smaller, smallest
3. long, longest
4. strong, strongest
5. funnier, funniest
6. cold, colder
7. fat, fattest
8. high, higher

Page 69
1. race
2. throws
3. swim
4. begs
5. listens
6. writes
7. fall
8. works
9. sleeps
10. fly

Page 70
1. walk
2. sail
3. chases
4. likes
5. sit
6. builds
7. helps
8. eat

Page 71
1. helped
2. wished
3. saved
4. baked
5. planted
6. hurried
7. rolled
8. fried
9. twirled
10. carried
11. walked
12. wanted
13. liked
14. moved
15. worked
16. laughed

Page 72
1. danced
2. hoped
3. married
4. watched
5. washed
6. climbed
7. sharpened
8. moved

Page 73
1. passing
2. joking
3. jumping
4. raining
5. waiting
6. using
7. cleaning
8. saving
9. staying
10. mixing
11. hoping
12. helping
13. moving
14. staring
15. chewing
16. showing

Page 74
1. helping
2. spending
3. looking
4. parking
5. baking
6. recycling
7. riding
8. talking

Page 75
1. played
2. gnaw
3. cheers
4. rushing
5. march
6. reading
7. crying
8. hoped

Answer Key

Page 76
1. gallop, gallops
2. walking, walked
3. clean, cleaning
4. sits
5. writing, write
6. roasted
7. learned, learning
8. lift, lifts
9. color
10. wait, waited

Page 77
1. turn, call, jump, point
2. whistle, skate, paint
3. a 4. b 5. b 6. a
7. a 8. a 9. b 10. b

Page 78
1. run
2. wrote
3. said
4. see
5. came
6. come
7. write
8. sat

Page 79
1. are
2. is
3. are
4. is
5. am
6. are
7. is
8. Is
9. am
10. is
11. are
12. are
13. Are
14. is
15. are
16. are

Page 80
1. is, are
2. are
3. is, are
4. am, are
5. am
6. is, are
7. is
8. Are
9. is, are
10. are, is

Page 81
1. do
2. does
3. does
4. do
5. do
6. Do
7. does
8. does
9. Does
10. does

Page 82
1. has
2. have
3. have
4. has
5. has
6. has
7. has
8. has
9. have

Page 83
1. have, has
2. have, has
3. has
4. has, have
5. has, have
6. has, have
7. has
8. have
9. Has, Have
10. has

Page 84
1. was
2. were
3. were
4. were
5. was
6. was
7. were
8. was
9. was

Page 85
1. was, were
2. was
3. was, were
4. was, were
5. Were
6. were, was
7. were, was
8. was
9. were
10. were, was

Page 86
1. seen
2. seen
3. seen
4. saw
5. seen
6. saw
7. saw
8. seen
9. saw
10. seen

Page 87
1. had, have
2. do, did
3. did, does
4. had, has
5. had, has
6. did, do

Page 88
1. saw, seen
2. do, does
3. were
4. do, did
5. am
6. has, had
7. has, have
8. are, is
9. is, are
10. are

Page 89
1. loudly
2. quietly
3. slowly
4. noisily
5. fiercely
6. brightly
7. carefully
8. proudly
9. quickly
10. rapidly

Page 90
(Answers may vary.)
1. quickly
2. loudly
3. politely
4. slowly
5. badly
6. smoothly
7. peacefully
8. silently
9. softly

Page 91
1. a 2. a 3. b 4. a 5. b
6. b 7. a 8. a 9. b 10. a
11. b 12. a 13. a 14. b

Page 92
1. Dad is going to cook hot dogs.
2. Julie found her lost book.
3. I feed my pet hamster every day.
4. Tom was the first one in line.
5. The pig played in the mud.
6. The boy slipped on the ice.
7. I wish I could fly like a bird.
8. We visited the farmer's market.

Page 93
1. A bud
2. Matthew
3. The second grade class
4. A tiny ant
5. I
6. The clock
7. Seven goldfish
8. The little girl
9. A wicked witch

Page 94
1. c 2. f 3. g 4. a
5. h 6. b 7. e 8. d
9-10. (Subjects will vary.)

Page 95
1. Flies and bees buzz.
2. Dogs and cats run.
3. Girls and boys play soccer.
4. Rain and wind ruined the picnic.
5. Lisa and Robby painted a picture.
6. Mom and I washed the dishes.

Answer Key

Page 96
1. screwed the bolts in tightly.
2. shook the sky.
3. won the spelling bee.
4. erupted from the volcano.
5. broke Mom's favorite vase.
6. played kickball.
7. drove us to school this morning.
8. changed the flat tire.
9. rang.

Page 97
(Answers may vary.)
1. rode a camel.
2. blew the man's hat.
3. eats a good breakfast.
4. live in a castle.
5. chose a good book.
6. watered the garden.
7. packed his suitcase for the trip.
8. claps his hands.

Page 98
1. Mary coughs and sneezes.
2. My dog barks and begs.
3. The glass fell and broke.
4. The giant shouts and roars.
5. The band plays and marches.
6. Leaves change color and fall.

Page 99
1. We skated on the frozen pond.
2. Jake and Todd play a card game.
3. The little girl dreamed about a magical fairy.
4. Snails and turtles move slowly.
5. The acrobats and the clowns performed perfectly.
6. The explorers discovered a new island.
7. Grandma baked a cake and a pie.
8. A hungry caterpillar ate through a leaf.
9. The rainstorm destroyed the roof on the house.
10. People listened to the orchestra music.

Page 100
(Invitations will vary.)

Page 101
(Letters will vary.)

Page 102
1. Linda
2. Ally
3. going to the zoo
(Letters will vary.)

Page 103
1. sailboat
2. shoelace
3. campfire
4. haircut
5. sandbox
6. scarecrow
7. railroad
8. toothbrush

Page 104
1. flashlight
2. skateboard
3. sunburn
4. doghouse
5. strawberry
6. seashells
7. fireplace
8. sunshine
9. mailbox
10. snowflakes

Page 105
1. d   2. b   3. g   4. i   5. a
6. e   7. j   8. c   9. h   10. f

Page 106
1. he's
2. we're
3. I'll
4. couldn't
5. they've
6. isn't
7. you're
8. didn't
9. We are
10. Let us
11. They are
12. Are not

Page 107
(Order of answers 1-6 may vary.)
1. birthday   2. paintbrush
3. butterfly   4. scarecrow
5. snowman   6. something
7. d   8. b   9. a
10. b   11. d   12. b

Page 108
1. glad
2. sick
3. large
4. make
5. quick
6. small
7. close
8. story
9. yell
10. sleep
11. angry
12. present
13. bucket
14. home
15. car
16. jump
17. raise
18. rock

Page 109
1. sound
2. quick
3. giggle
4. tiny
5. pal
6. nice
7. start
8. above
9. hope
10. easy

Page 110
1. hot
2. long
3. awake
4. full
5. slow
6. white
7. down
8. wet
9. sad
10. last
11. old
12. wide
13. stop
14. hard
15. go
16. low
17. dirty
18. rich

Page 111
1. close
2. short
3. hot
4. well
5. few
6. day
7. sit
8. strong
9. float
10. front

Page 112
1. sun/son
2. meet/meat
3. road/rode
4. sail/sale
5. tail/tale
6. see/sea
7. ate/eight
8. toe/tow

Page 113
1. blew, blue
2. hear, here
3. tale, tail
4. heel, heal
5. maid, made
6. rode, road
7. ate, eight
8. dear, deer
9. see, sea
10. two, too

Answer Key

Page 114
1. c	2. a	3. b	4. c
5. a	6. a	7. c	8. b
9. b	10. a	11. b	12. c
13. c	14. c	15. a	16. a
17. c	18. c	19. a	20. b
21. b	22. a	23. c	24. b

Page 115
1. reread – read again
2. remake – make again
3. retry – try again
4. replay – play again
5. repack – pack again
6. reheat – heat again
7. retie – tie again
8. rewrite – write again

Page 116
1. unhappy – not happy
2. undressed – not dressed
3. unlucky – not lucky
4. unlocked – not locked
5. unripe – not ripe
6. unwrapped – not wrapped
7. unsafe – not safe
8. unopened – not opened

Page 117
1. graceful – full of grace
2. useful – full of use
3. tearful – full of tears
4. playful – full of plays
5. joyful
6. helpful
7. careful
8. wonderful

Page 118
1. painless, hopeless, colorless, nameless
2. hopeless   3. nameless
4. painless   5. colorless
6. homeless

Page 119
1. surely, roughly, brightly, sadly
2. brightly   3. surely
4. roughly   5. sadly
6. slowly

Page 120
1. rewrite, unhappy, unsure, redraw, redo
2. unwrap, unpack, recheck, unafraid
3. helpful, powerful, toothless, slowly
4. likely, useful, grateful, neatly, wordless
5. neatly   6. repay   7. unopened
8. hopeful   9. unable   10. painless

Page 121
1. boat, plane, ride, train
2. bench, fun, shell, waves
3. chase, jump, march, poke
4. Earth, Mars, Saturn, Venus
5. acrobat, circus, horse, paint
6. dark, moon, night, star
7. friends, pencil, teacher, work
8. juice, lemonade, milk, soda
9. bolt, hammer, nail, screw

Page 122
From top to bottom, the numbers read:
1. 2, 1, 3	2. 3, 1, 2
3. 2, 3, 1	4. 1, 2, 3
5. 2, 3, 1	6. 2, 3, 1
7. 1, 3, 2	8. 1, 3, 2
9. 3, 1, 2	10. 2, 3, 1
11. 2, 3, 1	12. 1, 3, 2
13. 3, 2, 1	14. 1, 2, 3
15. 3, 1, 2	16. 1, 3, 2
17. 1, 3, 2	18. 2, 3, 1
19. 1, 2, 3	20. 2, 1, 3
21. 2, 1, 3	22. 1, 3, 2
23. 3, 2, 1	24. 1, 3, 2

Page 123
2., 4., 5., 6., 9., 10., 12., 13., 15., 17., 18., 19., 22., 23., 25.

Page 124
From top to bottom, the numbers read:
5, 3, 1, 4, 2

Page 125
From top to bottom, the numbers read:
4, 1, 6, 2, 5, 3

Page 126
1. b	2. a	3. b	4. b
5. a	6. b	7. b	8. a

Page 127
1. Melanie and Barb will go swimming.
2. Grandma and Mom will bake a strawberry pie.
3. Jerry will call the fire department.

Page 128
1. Our family loves to go to the movies.
2. There is so much to do at the campground.
3. The kitchen was a mess!
4. I had a hard time waking up this morning.

Page 129
1. b   2. c   3. a

Page 130
1. The family had a picnic last night.
2. The picnic was in their yard.
3. They ate hot dogs, cheese, and fruit.
4. They played hide-and-seek.
5. They went inside when it got dark.

Answer Key

Page 131
1. Dill was a big dinosaur.
2. The cave was in the deepest part of the forest.
3. It was quiet with yummy trees to nibble on.
4. He felt lonely.
5. A new family moving in.

Page 132
Adam: 2., 8., 10.
Kevin: 4., 5., 6.
Both: 1., 3., 7., 9.

Page 133
1. a 3. b 5. a
2. a 4. b 6. b

Page 134
1. a crayon   2. boots
3. baseball   4. a stamp
5. a kite   6. a doctor

Page 135
1. Mom went to the grocery store.
2. The man took our picture.
3. Fall is here.
4. Ian is playing soccer.

Page 136
1. a 2. c 3. b 4. a 5. c

Page 137
1. David, birds, David's friends
2. David
3. young, happy, surprised, a boy

Page 138
1. he won the race.
2. because he lost his bone.
3. Robin went sledding.
4. because she got a nice gift.
5. Lila wore a raincoat.
6. because Jenny gave it water.
7. because he called his brother a name.
8. many people like him.

Page 139
1. He wanted fish for lunch.
2. Jordan didn't catch the ball.
3. They eat harmful insects.
4. He got a good grade.

Page 140
1. Jumping rope is good exercise.
2. A baseball team has nine players.
3. A rose is a flower.
4. Dogs cannot climb trees.
5. This store sells ice cream.
6. This cap costs five dollars.

Page 141
1. F 2. O 3. O 4. F
5. O 6. F 7. F 8. F

Page 142
1. c 2. a 3. c 4. a

Page 143
1. b 5. c 9. b
2. a 6. a 10. d
3. d 7. a 11. b
4. c 8. c 12. a

Page 144
1. b 7. a
2. c 8. b
3. b 9. d
4. a 10. c
5. c 11. a
6. b

Page 145
1. a 2. a 3. b 4. a
5. c 6. a 7. a 8. b

Page 146
1. b 4. b 7. b
2. a 5. c 8. a
3. c 6. a

Page 147
1. c 5. c
2. a 6. b
3. b 7. a
4. a 8. c

Page 148
1. b 4. b 7. c
2. c 5. a 8. b
3. a 6. c

Page 149
1. c 4. c
2. a 5. b
3. b 6. a

Page 150
1. b 5. b 9. c
2. c 6. a 10. a
3. a 7. c 11. c
4. d 8. d 12. b

Page 151
1. a 2. b 3. a
4. b 5. b 6. a
7. b 8. b 9. a
10. a 11. a 12. b

Page 152
1. c 2. b 3. a 4. b 5. b